Jessa ha *intently, staring into his eyes as if she were searching for something.*

As if she were searching for something she thought she should find.

Something familiar.

He'd stopped breathing for a moment, wondering if somehow, some way, she had recognized him. And his heart gave a ridiculous leap as if, impossibly, in hope. He'd sneered at himself the instant he recognized the long-lost emotion.

He didn't indulge in hope. It accomplished nothing, helped nothing, saved nothing.

He'd had to fight down the urge to tell her.

Dear Reader,

There are times, as a writer, when you regret having created a certain character. When you wish you'd spent less time on them. When you wish you hadn't built them up quite so much. When you're flat-out afraid that when their story rolls around, you won't do them justice after all the preamble.

Enter the mysterious man known as St. John. Of all the characters of Redstone, Incorporated, other than Josh Redstone himself, St. John has generated the most reaction, the most mail, the most requests for his story. So naturally, my reaction was to stall. Wait. Tell myself I'd know when the time was right. Yeah, that's it, I wasn't really afraid, it just wasn't time yet.

When I sat down to finally face the man and realized why he was the way he was, I wasn't afraid anymore. I was terrified. But he wouldn't budge, wouldn't allow me to shortchange him, coddle him or in any way clean up his life. It all had to be there, because it was what made him who he was.

So for all of you who have wondered and, thank you, cared, here at last is his story.

My best to you all,

Justine Davis

JUSTINE DAVIS

The Best Revenge

Silhouette®

Romantic
SUSPENSE

If you purchased this book without a cover you should be aware
that this book is stolen property. It was reported as "unsold and
destroyed" to the publisher, and neither the author nor the
publisher has received any payment for this "stripped book."

SILHOUETTE BOOKS

Recycling programs
for this product may
not exist in your area.

ISBN-13: 978-0-373-27667-7

THE BEST REVENGE

Copyright © 2010 by Janice Davis Smith

All rights reserved. Except for use in any review, the reproduction
or utilization of this work in whole or in part in any form by any
electronic, mechanical or other means, now known or hereafter
invented, including xerography, photocopying and recording, or in
any information storage or retrieval system, is forbidden without
the written permission of the editorial office, Silhouette Books,
233 Broadway, New York, NY 10279 U.S.A.

This is a work of fiction. Names, characters, places and incidents are
either the product of the author's imagination or are used fictitiously, and
any resemblance to actual persons, living or dead, business establishments,
events or locales is entirely coincidental.

This edition published by arrangement with Harlequin Books S.A.

® and TM are trademarks of Harlequin Books S.A., used under license.
Trademarks indicated with ® are registered in the United States Patent
and Trademark Office, the Canadian Trade Marks Office and in other
countries.

Visit Silhouette Books at www.eHarlequin.com

Printed in U.S.A.

Books by Justine Davis

Silhouette Romantic Suspense

JUSTINE DAVIS

lives on Puget Sound in Washington. Her interests outside of writing are sailing, doing needlework, horseback riding and driving her restored 1967 Corvette roadster—top down, of course.

Justine says that years ago, during her career in law enforcement, a young man she worked with encouraged her to try for a promotion to a position that was at the time occupied only by men. "I succeeded, became wrapped up in my new job, and that man moved away, never, I thought, to be heard from again. Ten years later he appeared out of the woods of Washington State, saying he'd never forgotten me and would I please marry him. With that history, how could I write anything but romance?"

and it had worked well in initial trials, was ready for testing

Chapter 1

"Coward."

St. John looked at himself in the mirror. The scar was less vivid than usual this morning, perhaps because there wasn't much tan to contrast with the thin, long ridge that slashed along the right side of his jaw. That happened when you hid inside most of the time, he told himself.

Coward was definitely the word, he added silently.

He'd been hiding more than usual lately. Not that there had been more problems at Redstone. The opposite in fact; things were going well on all fronts. The Hawk V jet was ready for delivery. The damage done by the snake in their midst at Research and Development was finally under control, losses minimized and security rebuilt. That had inspired their resident inventor to a new round of genius, including a couple of revolutionary concepts that had made even Josh Redstone blink; the idea of an implanted microchip to help stroke victims with residual tremors would never have occurred to him as a Redstone offshoot. But Ian Gamble had done it, and it had worked well in initial trials, was ready for further testing. Josh's philosophy of hiring the best continued to pay off; Redstone's people were its true strength.

Unfortunately for St. John, they were also the problem. Not that there was anything wrong with them. To the contrary, they were indeed the best. And happy. Very happy. Deliriously happy.

Of late, annoyingly happy.

If I have to go to one more Redstone wedding.... He couldn't even finish the thought.

It wasn't that he begrudged them. He'd made peace long ago with the fact that such things were not for him. It was simply that he didn't like the unaccustomed ache he'd begun to feel at the seemingly endless line of successful Redstone relationships and weddings. Even Redstone kids were starting to appear. And the only good thing he found in it all for himself was a bitter sort of thankfulness that none of them would ever face what he'd once faced.

"Add *whiner* to that *coward*," he muttered aloud, aware even as he said it that doing so spoke volumes about his state of mind; most of the time he barely spoke to other people, let alone himself.

He glanced at his watch as he pulled it on: 4:30 a.m. He was running a bit late. But it had been peaceful for weeks now, no late-night calls from some far-flung outpost of the Redstone empire, from people looking for help, information or advice. Just as well, he didn't like delving into those interpersonal situations that popped up anyway. Business situations were just that; the personal problems dragged emotions into it, which was the moment when he wanted out.

But now that he was out, for the time being anyway, he found himself oddly unsettled. He had the unwelcome feeling that helping Redstone people with their personal problems had been his substitute for human contact, and when that was gone…

Be careful what you wish for.

The old axiom had never held much water with him,

since he'd painfully learned at an early age that wishing accomplished nothing. If it had, he'd have wished himself away back then.

He ran his fingers through his still-damp hair. Haircut, he noted, mentally filing the task. Of course, he'd noted it daily since it started to brush past his collar, but since it would require a visit to the barbershop down the street, and Willis could talk like nobody else he knew, he kept putting it off.

He wasn't in the mood for chatter. An observation that anyone at Redstone would laugh at; as if he ever was. He knew the joke that had become a Redstone staple: "Why use one word when none will do?" What had begun as self-protection as a child had become a long-ingrained habit at thirty-five, and he didn't see the need to change it. He got his job done, and well, that was what mattered.

He took the stairs down to the next level, even though his legs were still a bit tired from his pre-dawn workout. Another habit ingrained long ago: if you ever had to run, it helped if you could.

His spacious office was on the west side of Redstone Headquarters. In the early morning darkness, the spread of lights below from this floor was impressive. Distracting, but impressive. The wall of glass was treated with Ian Gamble's special anti-glare coating that allowed full visibility yet made it possible to easily read each of the computer monitors behind him even in full daylight.

He settled into what Josh laughingly called his battle station. He supposed it looked like one, this U-shaped arrangement with the bank of four monitors on one side, the multiline phone he'd customized to his needs—from anonymous lines to lines labeled with various useful names and locations—on the next and the actual desk on the last.

He would have preferred having his back to the expansive view, which included a distant glimpse of the Pacific, but the office designer had assumed whoever would occupy this office would, of course, want the view.

A reasonable assumption, he told himself as he sat down. For anyone else.

He booted up the bank of computers. One was connected to the Redstone internal network, but the others were his own, independent and carefully secured. Not to protect the data on them, not here inside Redstone, but to protect Redstone from his less traditional methods of inquiry.

He was finalizing his attack plan for the day when a quiet beep alerted him that his news-tracking program had posted an alert. The Gordon merger, he thought as he turned to look at the screen. Or maybe a development in Arethusa, the Caribbean island in close proximity to the Redstone Bay Resort; the self-styled rebels who were in truth drug traffickers were getting restless again. So far it wasn't serious as far as Redstone was concerned, but—

The brief abstract on the automated search return sat there quietly, dark letters on a glowing screen. Some part of his mind, the part not blasted into numbness, registered that the sky had lightened. But that was in the periphery. His focus was on the words on the screen.

It was a simple enough announcement. It would seem unimportant to most in the Redstone world, indeed, in the entire world. After all, what did it matter who chose to run for mayor of a little town like Cedar, Oregon?

It shouldn't matter to you, either.

The stern voice in his head brought him back to his surroundings. The chill faded.

It didn't matter. Not after all these years.

He shut the alert window. Turned back to his work. Wondered once more if he should just bite the bullet and have this whole battle station turned around so he wouldn't have to face the sunrise every day. Josh wouldn't care, he knew that. Except perhaps to comment, in that low, slow drawl that tended to fool foolish people into thinking his mind was slow, as well, that turning his back on the world wouldn't make it go away.

True. But he could pretend for a while.

And ignore the fact that that had never helped all those years ago, either.

Jessa had heard the rumblings weeks ago, when the town council had finally announced the upcoming special election, but had been too busy to pay much attention. Keeping Hill Feed and Supply going took most of her time and energy, and her mother and dog used up the rest. She wasn't complaining. In fact, she was glad of the dawn-to-dark busyness; it kept her from constantly thinking about how much she missed her dad.

But now it appeared the rumblings were official.

"Everybody in town loves you," Marion Wagman said enthusiastically. "Always have."

Well, no, Jessa thought as she lifted the last bag of dog food onto the shelf. Jim Stanton came to mind. She could laugh about it now, but at the time, her senior year in high school, it had stung that his need to be out of small-town life far surpassed his desire to be with her.

"It would be a given," Marion was saying. "Your name is all it would take."

Jessa listened only absently as she considered her progress; she now tossed around forty-pound bags of dog food and managed even heavier bags of livestock feed with at least some amount of ease. A far cry from when she'd had to take over eight months ago.

Jessa smothered a sigh as she pushed her bangs off her forehead. She'd long ago cut her blond locks gamine short for convenience, but keeping it in any kind of shape sometimes seemed to take more time than when she'd had hair halfway down her back. And time was something she had too little of these days.

"You can't really want your father's office to go to someone else."

Marion's voice had taken on a tone of determination Jessa

had learned well when the woman had been her ninth-grade history teacher. That's what this was, she thought. The woman just liked history, and since a Hill had been in the mayor's office for nearly four decades, the idea of having another appealed to her. Never mind that Jessa barely had time to breathe, let alone take on something as time-consuming as what Marion was proposing. Even if she wanted to. Which she didn't.

"It's not my father's office, and it wasn't my grandfather's," she said. "It's the mayor's office. It belongs to whoever is elected."

And the idea of that being her was beyond absurd. Her father had been wonderful at it because he'd had the respect and liking of almost the entire population of Cedar—all nine thousand of them—for nearly thirty years.

But he'd had a knack she'd never had, and frankly never wanted. How many times as a child had she grown impatient with the fact that they couldn't simply walk down the street from the post office to the library without him being stopped a dozen times by people who wanted to thank, gripe to, congratulate or simply chat with their personal and personable mayor? While she, after the expected adult-to-child patter, was mostly ignored?

The ignoring part actually suited her fine; in her mind she was already in the library, picking out the books that would teach and transport her for weeks on end. She'd learn how to teach a horse to do a flying change of leads, and how to stop her otherwise perfect dog, Kula, from carrying home—completely unharmed—Mr. Carpenter's pet pigeons, and then she'd get lost in the latest visit to her favorite literary fantasy kingdom.

"You're the only one who can do this, Jessa," Marion was saying now. "People will vote for you because you're your father's girl. You're the only one who can beat him."

Jessa stopped then, the clipboard she'd just made a note

on—her father had been resistant to a completely computerized system—still in her hands.

"You have something against Mr. Alden?" she asked carefully.

"I just think a Hill should continue as our mayor." Marion dismissed Jessa's cautious question with a wave.

"There's always Uncle Larry," Jessa said.

Marion's eyes widened, and Jessa smothered a smile. Her uncle, who lived in the small cottage on the edge of town that was known mainly for the swarm of garden gnomes that infested his yard, was known in turn to be slightly…eccentric. Oddly wise, but definitely eccentric.

"Can you imagine how quiet council meetings would be, waiting to see what he'd say?" Jessa said.

The mere thought accomplished what Jessa hadn't yet been able to do; Marion made her excuses and left the store.

Jessa went back to work, focusing on the next task, restocking the salt blocks. Doc Halperin, the local vet, would be needing them for his horses. She ignored the glass case beside the shelves, and the glitter and colors, mostly blue, of the trophies and ribbons inside. She'd often told her father they should remove it for a bit more valuable sales space in the already crowded store. The mementos of her glory days on the local horse show circuit were ancient history now, she'd said. But he'd been steadfast, proud of her success, perhaps even more than she had been.

She could change it now, she thought once more. He wasn't here to nix her suggestions anymore. Not that he had rejected all of them. He'd okayed her idea to add the line of horse-themed greeting cards done by a local artist who also happened to be an old classmate of hers, in a rack by the cash register where people had time to look as they waited for their purchases to be rung up. Their success had pleased her nearly as much as that state championship cup and ribbon, because she'd had to convince her dad to do it and had been proven right.

Yes, she could change anything she wanted now, do all the things she'd wanted to when he was here and, in her eyes, too slow to embrace change. But now that her father was gone, she perversely clung to things exactly as they were, as if changing anything would be an insult to his memory.

Or admitting he's really gone, she thought.

The ache she hadn't found a way to avoid built up in her. Quickly, her mind tried to dodge the pain, and the first haven she found was Marion Wagman's ridiculous suggestion. It was funny, really, and it would be nice to smile instead of cry.

However, the now officially declared candidacy of Albert Alden put a hitch in the whole gallop, she thought. And now that her father was gone, he was smugly assuming no one would dare oppose him, and that the election was a mere formality. It was also because, unlike the seeming majority of Cedar residents, she didn't have a stellar opinion of the smoothest man in town. Alden might be wealthy—he certainly was by Cedar standards—and polished, and have a fancy degree from an elite eastern college on his office wall, but Jessa knew there was more, under the surface. Much more.

Problem was, she was probably the only one in town who didn't believe the man's polished exterior, artfully tinged with a practiced sadness over the tragedies in his life, went any deeper than his bright, white smile.

So, isn't that practically a requirement for a politician? she asked herself rhetorically.

But the joke sounded feeble even in her head. Especially when stacked up against what she knew about Cedar's most well-known pillar of the community. That she couldn't prove any of it didn't change the slight nausea she felt, even after all these years. And part of it was guilt; she'd only been a child at the time, but she still felt she should have done something. That the one who had the biggest stake in it begged her not to say a word was the only thing that had kept her silent.

But now she was an adult. And surely there was no statute

of limitations on such things? But with the victim long dead, what could she do now?

What should she do?

Could she really stand by and let the man sail into the office her father, and his father before him, had held with such dignity and honor? Could she stay silent, suspecting what she did, even if she couldn't prove it? Just whispering her suspicions against a man with his standing would not only be useless, but probably earn her astonished disbelief.

And with that, she arrived at the bottom line.

Could she let her beloved hometown put Albert Alden in charge of Cedar's six schools, when her deepest, most silent suspicion was that he would abuse the power in the worst possible way?

She sank down to sit on the crate of salt blocks.

"No," she whispered to the empty store. "I can't. I just can't."

But she wasn't sure if she meant she couldn't afford to try to stop him, or couldn't afford not to.

Chapter 2

"You what?"

Josh was looking at him as if he were a jet engine that had suddenly meowed.

"You heard me," St. John said. He was so full of reluctance, disquiet and anger at himself for not being able to let this go, that he was sure he sounded more like a junkyard dog growling.

"Why?"

"By my calculations I have 333.6 vacation days coming," he said, giving his boss and the head of Redstone something he rarely graced others with; full sentences.

"Which I know darn well and doesn't answer the question." Josh shot the response back with narrowed eyes, and St. John knew his effort to avoid a direct answer had done the opposite of what he'd hoped. Instead of diverting Josh, he'd sharpened his attention. And that, St. John thought wearily, was the last thing he'd wanted.

"Saying no?"

Josh leaned back in his chair. "You've known me since

you were a teenager," he said after a moment. "You know better."

He did know better. He'd just been hoping Josh would let this go without prying into the reasons. A fruitless hope, he realized when the man who never missed a thing slowly unfurled his lanky body from the big leather chair.

"You're also my right-hand man, as close to indispensable as anyone is at Redstone, including me. Redstone wouldn't be what it is without you."

St. John didn't politely protest the statement; he knew he was damned good at what he did, even if there was no formal job description behind his rarely used official title of Vice President of Operations. Mainly because, as Josh's personal pilot Tess Machado often said, it would take the *Oxford English Dictionary* to hold it.

"I owe you all the time you could want, even though your absence will have a tremendous impact. But none of that matters," Josh added as St. John remained mute.

The silence spun out long enough to make most people edgy. But silence was his preferred default, so he had no problem simply waiting for Josh to get to whatever he was going to say. Finally Josh's mouth twitched at the corners, and St. John knew he'd given in with his usual amusement.

"What matters," Josh said as if the long pause had never happened, "is that my right-hand man, who hasn't taken a single vacation day in over a decade, who lives upstairs so he can sneak into work on holidays, I suspect even Christmas, suddenly wants time off."

"Yes or no?" St. John asked gruffly.

For another long moment Josh just looked at him. St. John wasn't intimidated that his boss topped his just under six-foot height by a good three inches. Or maybe it was just that Josh never tried to intimidate with his size; it was all part of his highly successful approach of letting the people who didn't know better think of him as some stupid hick with a country-fried accent right up until they realized they'd been bested by a master.

When he spoke again, it was almost a whisper. "And if I said no?"

I'd be relieved, St. John thought. *Glad of the excuse not to go.*

And that admission, even inwardly, rattled him. Hadn't he learned the hard way that avoiding reality never worked? It was what it was, and you either dealt with it or you didn't, but it never changed. And not dealing with it, not facing it, hadn't been an option since he was seven.

"Won't," he finally muttered, lapsing into his usual monosyllabic response style.

"No," Josh said with a sigh, "I won't say no. But at least tell me where you'll be. You're the only one at Redstone who could step in if anything happened to me."

"Won't. Draven."

Josh lifted a brow, indicating he'd noticed the retreat into nonconversational mode, but he didn't press.

"Yes, thanks to John and his people I'm as safe as I can be. But that doesn't change the fact that I may need to reach you. Where will you be?"

St. John reached into a pocket and pulled out his customized, Redstone-built smart phone, an intricate, multifunction pocket computer with global communication capabilities, presenting rather than speaking the answer.

Josh let out a wry chuckle. "I know it's hard for your technological mind to accept, but there actually are places where that baby of yours won't work."

"Shudder," St. John said.

Josh blinked. "A joke? You made a joke? Now I'm really worried."

St. John lowered his eyes. "Don't."

Josh went very still, abandoning even the pretense of humor. "Dam," he said, using the shortened version of St. John's rarely used and hastily chosen first name, Dameron.

The world insisted he have a last and first name, and at the time he hadn't wanted to draw the attention not having one would, so he'd picked one in much the same manner he'd chosen St. John.

St. John waited. Silently.

"I've never pressed you on anything you didn't want to talk about," Josh said. "Which means nearly everything."

"More than most," he muttered.

"Maybe I do know more than most, but that only means they know nothing. That's not the point. You can't just ask for time off for nearly the first time in history, tell me nothing and expect me not to wonder, if not worry."

St. John resisted the urge to run. He was feeling the pressure this man, unlike any other on the planet, could exert on him without even trying, simply by virtue of the fact that had it not been for Josh Redstone's appearance in his life those many years ago, he'd be dead. And despite the moments when he slipped into the old habit of thinking he'd be better off that way, one thing never changed.

I won't give him the satisfaction.

The mantra aimed at the demon who had set the course of his life from the day he was born was old, well used, but no less powerful than it had ever been. The fact that that evil walking would never know how badly he'd failed, never know that the son he'd tried to destroy had not just survived, but managed in his own way to thrive, didn't matter. St. John knew.

"Where are you going?"

The question was quiet, even gentle. And this was Josh, the man who had made it possible for him to turn the tables, to prove the dire predictions wrong. He deserved an answer. He even deserved the truth.

St. John drew in a breath. With an effort he didn't like admitting it took, he met those steady gray eyes. And the word he'd resisted saying, or even thinking, for twenty years came out.

"Home," he said.

* * *

In the early-morning light, Jessa sat in her father's big, leather chair, Maui sprawled at—or rather on—her feet. She took comfort from the dog's warmth as she stared at the school yearbook in her lap.

She both liked and hated sitting here; sometimes she swore she could catch a whiff of her father's aftershave, and if she was deep into something her subconscious processed that spiced scent into his presence. And that made returning to the reality of his forever absence even more of a jolt. It also made her decision, when her father had become ill, to temporarily move back into the house she'd grown up in both the worst and best of her life.

She turned the page of the yearbook. It wasn't the formal, posed portraits of the students she was looking for. In that shot, the son of the man who would be mayor looked just like the rest of the boys in his class, stiff, overly tidy and uncomfortable. But in the section rather grandly labeled "campus life," she found the photograph she remembered. A large group of kids, laughing, sitting in a loose circle on the grassy quad area of the school. And off to one side, barely in focus, a lone, dark-haired boy sat looking at the group with an expression she'd never been able to quite decide on. Was it envy? Dislike? Longing? All she knew for sure was that he was not part of that group.

Adam Alden never had been.

She'd never been quite able to figure out the why of that, either. Was it that his father was a successful attorney, with two offices in this rural county? Was it envy on the part of those kids that kept him isolated? She couldn't see it; Adam had never lorded it over anyone, in fact, he often did without the latest, greatest craze item that others had, his father saying he was making sure he didn't grow up spoiled.

Back then she had, with all the intensity of a very bright ten-year-old, decided that it was Adam himself who kept his distance. It wasn't that this group was a clique who kept others out: Adam just stayed apart from everyone. That made many feel he was aloof, or even weird. Jessa had just thought him sad. But she knew more than most, despite the fact that she had been nearly five years younger.

She had never been sure what had drawn the fourteen-year-old back again and again, after that first chance meeting in her special place along the river. Nor had she ever been sure what it was about her that had made him talk to her the way he had. Perhaps, she'd thought when she herself had turned fourteen, it had been that there were few things less threatening than a ten-year-old girl. Or perhaps it had been simply that she listened, both fascinated and aching inside, offering the only thing she could, quiet support and refuge.

Yes, she knew more. She had wrestled with her suspicions, trying with all her ten-year-old earnestness to decide if she should violate the promise of silence she'd made to the dark-haired boy with the vivid—and haunted—blue eyes.

And then the hundred-years storm had hit, young Adam Alden was dead, and none of it seemed to matter anymore.

She didn't have the heart to do what she usually did, go to the shelf and pull out her own elementary school yearbook, the one that he'd signed for her, just days before he'd died. She didn't need to look; the words he'd written had been seared into her mind for two decades now.

Jess— To the brightest place in this dark world. A.

He'd been the only one allowed to call her that. Jess was her father, and while she was thrilled to have been named after him, the shortened form of Jesse was his alone. But when Adam used it she liked it, as if it were something personal, private between them, shared with no one else.

Maui stirred, letting out a sigh that told her that while he'd patiently wait until she was done, he'd much rather be outside chasing whatever she'd throw for him until her arm ached. Which was exactly what she should do, before it got dark, instead of wasting time mulling over sad memories and useless should-haves.

"Come on, boy," she said, slapping the yearbook closed and returning it to the shelf; as mayor her father had received copies of every album from every school for every year, so although she'd been four years behind him in school, she'd been able to trace Adam Alden's progress and changes from an early age to this last yearbook, the last he would ever be in. That he was the only child among the half dozen people who had died in that horrible storm had made him, if not a legend, then at least the featured player in a tragic story of mythic proportions, by Cedar standards at least.

The big golden retriever scrambled to his feet, expressive brown eyes alight, plumed tail waving in hopeful excitement. As clearly as if he'd spoken, Jessa could hear the "Now? Now, Mom, can we play now?"

She reached to scratch behind the gentle dog's ears. If it wasn't for Maui, she could easily slide into a morass of grief so deep she'd never see daylight again. But the dog's quiet support and his need for attention and care had kept her going when the last thing she wanted was to get up and face another day. She even found a pained sort of comfort in his name, the latest in the Hawaiian name tradition started by her father because her parents had honeymooned in the islands.

"Come on, golden boy. Let's find a nice, grubby, slobbery tennis ball for you to chase."

The clever dog may not have understood everything, but "come on" and "ball" were all he needed to hear. He let out a happy yelp; all was now right with his world.

As she stood in the huge yard between the house and the back of the store, watching the tireless retriever retrieve and return for more, in the back of her mind was a silent apology to the loving, happy animal whose life she was about to turn upside down.

"Enjoy it while you can, boy," she whispered.

Because looking back at those pictures, at the flat, captured images of the boy who had been such a dramatic part of her life, who had told her things he'd told no one else, and who, in death, had become part of the lore of this small town she loved, had decided her.

There was no way she could let the man who had put the haunted, hunted look in Adam Alden's eyes—and the bruises on his body—take charge of this town without a fight.

Chapter 3

St. John drove slowly. He was able to tell himself it wasn't reluctance, it was because the speed limit was twenty-five, and Cedar's single assigned deputy—at least, that's all there had been twenty years ago—liked to sit in a turnout just beyond the city limits and wait for those who didn't slow down in time.

But now there was a warning sign a good quarter mile ahead, telling drivers of the drop in speed limit on the two-lane road. And when he got there, no cop. Maybe somebody had listened to the complaints that it was a speed trap.

Common sense told him there would be many other changes, but he hadn't expected the next one he came across, literally; a new, sturdy, truss-style bridge over the Cedar River. Since the old bridge hadn't been that old, as bridges go, he wondered what had happened, wondered for a moment if it had been damaged in a flood. Perhaps even *that* flood. It wasn't like Cedar had a lot of money to throw around. Of course, it was a county road, so likely—

The disgusted realization that he was rambling in his head

to avoid thinking about where he was and why cut off his own thoughts.

He has no power over me anymore.

The words echoed in his head for the first time in a very long time. He'd begun chanting it at fourteen. By the time he'd turned twenty, thanks to Josh, he'd finally believed it.

So why are you acting like he does?

As the road rounded the final curve, he saw another addition; a large shopping center with a couple of major anchor stores. He vaguely remembered the hearty discussions about the proposed development all those years ago, with then mayor Jesse Hill as one of the strongest proponents. And he wondered if the increased tax revenue from the center had helped pay for the new bridge.

Mayor Hill.

Jessa's father.

He shook his head sharply. The man's death had, in a way, spurred all this, but he hadn't thought about it beyond that at first. He'd been focused on the man who wanted to replace him. But finally it had hit him, the personal cost of that death. To the one person in Cedar he'd let himself think about since the night he'd left it behind forever.

Jessa.

Logically, intellectually, he knew she must be devastated at losing the father she so loved, the man she'd been named after. He had no other way to look at it; he'd never known the kind of relationship they'd had. He'd marveled at it at fourteen, even been envious of the way she talked about her father as if he'd invented water. He'd tried to tell himself it was because she was so much younger, that things would change…but in his gut he'd known they wouldn't, that Jess Hill was as light, as true as his own father was dark and deceitful.

He had wondered if Jessa was even still here, or if she'd finally grown tired of small-town life and had moved on. She'd been a smart, wise-beyond-her-years child, someone he could easily imagine living a fast-paced, successful life in

a big city. But she'd loved Cedar and the more rural life, with
her horse, her dog and, as she'd put it even then, real dirt that
soaked up the rain, not concrete.

And if she was still here, and he ran into her...

He wasn't really worried she'd recognize him. No one
would. It had taken a few surgeries to repair the damage he'd
left Cedar with. His cheekbone, his crooked jaw. Even his
three-times-broken nose had been repaired and straightened,
so he could breathe normally, not because he gave a damn
what it looked like. And while they were at it, he'd had them
change a lot more, leaving only the scar he'd gained that night
as a reminder of his escape. There was very little left of that
kid who'd lived here.

No, not even Jessa would recognize him now. But wherever
she was, he wished her well. More than well. She'd saved him,
in her own way, much as Josh had. If he hadn't had her to talk
to—

He hit the brakes sharply enough that the seat belt locked
up to halt his forward momentum. Thankfully, despite the new
bridge and shopping center, there wasn't much traffic at this
time of day, and no one plowed into him from the rear after
the abrupt stop. He put the rental car in Reverse and backed
up and to the side of the road in one quick maneuver.

And on the small knoll beside the road was the answer
to all the questions he'd just been pondering. And the first
campaign sign he'd seen. But it was not for Albert Alden as
he'd expected.

It was for Jessa Hill.

"This is a bad thing, bad times."

Jessa sighed. She hadn't expected everyone to agree with
her decision, but she'd hoped at least her family would. Her
mother's objection, at least, she understood. She was afraid
Jessa was taking on too much, and Jessa herself wasn't sure
she wasn't right.

But her uncle seemed decided that this was a bad idea

for altogether different reasons. And whatever they were, Jessa figured she was about to hear them in his inimitable, seemingly scattered yet impossibly wise way. She tried to focus on her task, sorting through the store accounts. That computerized system was becoming a priority, she thought; doing this by hand as her father always had took far too much time. Just as her father had always given his regular customers too much time to pay without charging interest. But that wasn't a change she was willing to make; there was a reason people kept coming here instead of driving up the highway to the newer, bigger store twenty miles north.

"Sucking up everything in its path," her uncle said in one of his typical non sequiturs. It was too early in the morning, she thought, for her weary brain to try and follow his twisted path.

"But then," he added, "evil does."

Jessa blinked. She hadn't expected that one. The sheaf of monthly statements in her hand, she looked up at her uncle.

"Old man Alden would be spinning in his grave about now, to see this."

She guessed he was referring to the current Alden's grandfather, Clark Alden, who had died nearly twenty-five years ago. She'd only been five, but she remembered hearing her mother speak softly of Adam's pain over the loss of his great-grandfather, to whom he'd been close. She knew too well now that there was no comfort for that kind of pain.

She brought herself back to her uncle's words. "You mean, how dare I challenge his grandson?" she asked, remembering what little she'd known of the gruff old man.

"Backward, girl."

Her mouth twitched. "I'm going to assume that isn't a personal description."

Her uncle laughed. "You know better, girl. You're the brightest thing to ever come along in this family."

Thankfully, when it came to his love for her, her uncle's

frequent vagueness and cryptic observations became crystal clear. She smiled at him.

"Meant that old man Alden had a lot of respect for your dad. And our dad before that. Didn't care for politics himself."

She frowned. "You mean he wouldn't like the idea of his grandson as mayor?"

"He wouldn't like much about him, I'm afraid."

The regretful tone reminded Jessa of what he'd said a moment ago. "Evil, you said," she began.

"Maybe too strong," her uncle admitted, "but not by much."

For an instant Jessa's breath caught. Did he know? Could he suspect what she had long known? She hesitated before going on. "Do you think anyone in this town," she began carefully, "would believe that?"

He looked at her steadily, with that unnerving perceptiveness he often exhibited. "I think at least one might."

"Uncle Larry," she began, urgently now, but the sound of the front-door chime cut her off. She looked up through the small office window to see a man in a blue jacket, an old, gray wool driver's cap and the darkest sunglasses she'd ever seen standing just inside the door. His hair was dark and long enough to brush his collar. His jaw was unshaven, just short of stubbled, and he looked a little pale for the end of summer. She wondered if he'd been sick, or if she'd just gotten too used to the complexions of people who worked outside.

He was looking around, as people often did when they first came in; the store was comfortingly familiar to those who lived here and came in often, but to newcomers the plethora of goods was a bit overwhelming. The joke locally was you could find everything at Hill's, but you couldn't find anything. She'd floated the idea of organizing things a bit better with several of the most loyal customers, but the consensus—the rather vehement consensus—was that they liked things the way they were and rearranging it would only be more confusing.

After a moment the man began to walk purposefully, as if

he knew exactly where he was going. And apparently where he was going was here, she thought as he made his way straight toward her small office at the back of the store.

Jessa stood up; the stranger must need something in a hurry and was looking for someone to ask, she thought. She stepped to the office doorway just as he reached it.

"What can I help you find?" she asked in her best, helpful-proprietor tone.

For a long moment she found oddly strained, the man said nothing. He seemed to be staring at her, although she couldn't be sure with the dark glasses. Her gaze was drawn to a three-inch-long scar, thin and white, that ran along his jawbone on the right side. It looked old and rather jagged, as if the injury should have been stitched but wasn't.

"Most folks take those things off inside," her uncle said with a gesture at the sunglasses that obscured the man's eyes.

Jessa winced inwardly, hoping the stranger didn't take offense. Uncle Larry never did quite get the concept of tact with customers.

"Perhaps he needs them, Uncle Larry," she said, thinking he might have an eye problem that also explained the paleness. "Now, what can I help you with?"

The man still said nothing, but he did, after a moment's seeming hesitation, reach up and pull off the sunglasses.

The moment she saw his eyes, Jessa realized why he kept the shades on; it must be embarrassing to have everyone stop dead midsentence the moment you looked at them. Because if she hadn't already finished her sentence, that's what she would have done. Those piercing blue eyes made what had before been merely an interesting face absolutely riveting. It wasn't just the color, although that was striking enough, it was the sense that those eyes had seen more things than any five men, and too many of them not pleasant.

She gave herself a mental shake; she didn't usually fall into fanciful speculation about total strangers. But he was staring at her so intently, and it was giving her an odd feeling.

Ordinarily she would have thought it was simply a response to an attractive man, but this was something more. Something different.

"Can I help you?" She made the query again quickly, as much to shake off the odd effects as to get an answer.

He seemed, oddly, to relax slightly. As much as he probably ever did, she thought, judging by the air of tense readiness that seemed to cling to him. After a moment, he shook his head in answer to her question.

"Help you," he said.

She blinked. "Help me?"

He nodded toward the campaign sign in the office window, the only indication in the store that she was running; she didn't like the idea of cluttering up the place with reminders of what most folks in town already knew anyway.

"Make that happen," he said.

She didn't know if was something in the economy of his words or the flat, implacable confidence of his tone, but she knew he was utterly certain he could deliver on that promise.

What she didn't know about this dark, almost ominous stranger was why on earth he would.

Chapter 4

She hadn't recognized him.

He hadn't expected her to, yet he wouldn't have been surprised if somehow she had. That in itself surprised him, and warned him he'd better keep his guard up here in this place where old, creeping memories were stirring.

But he had recognized her immediately. She hadn't changed all that much, even if it had been twenty years, and she'd been only ten when he'd last seen her. Her hair was the same sunny blond that had tumbled down her back as a girl, although now it was cut short, in a tousled cap that suited her. It made her neck seem even more slender, and bared a delicate nape that belied her strength and made a man want to—

He cut off his own ridiculous thought with a jolt of shock. *That* was a road he had no business even looking at on a map, let alone considering traveling. This was Jessa, for God's sake, the girl who'd been like a sister to him.

But he couldn't help staring at those eyes, those wide, beautiful eyes the color of the river, and almost as changeable; green in some lights, hazel in others. They were still full of that wisdom, that sanity that had once been the only thing that had kept a struggling boy's head above water. He'd trusted her as much as he'd trusted anyone then, and she had never, ever let him down. And he hadn't found it odd that he trusted a girl almost five years younger than he, he'd only felt gratitude that there was anyone he could trust at all.

His throat tightened involuntarily. It was unsettling to realize that he was feeling...anything. He'd thought himself immune to even the harshest pressure of those memories, so thick and high was the wall he'd built around them.

Higher. Thicker, he told himself. He could do that without even thinking about it. Nothing could be harder than what it had taken to build those walls in the first place; adding to them would be easy, wouldn't distract at all from what he'd come here for.

"Fascinating."

The low murmur came from the man leaning against the doorjamb just behind Jessa. St. John flicked him a glance; he'd noticed the man, as he noticed everything, the moment he'd seen movement in the office at the back of the store. But now he placed him; Jessa's uncle, the oft-maligned but unexpectedly insightful Uncle Larry. He was grayer and heavier, but the sparkle was still in his green-gold eyes— Jessa's eyes—and his smile still had that fey sort of look that made people wonder just what he was seeing, and if it was of this world.

He gave that thought a fierce mental stomp; he had no time for such nonsense, let alone any inclination. Angry with himself, and not sure if it was for not being prepared for this, or for assuming he was, his voice was even more clipped than usual.

"Won't cut it," he said, gesturing at the discreet sign in the office window.

For an instant she drew back slightly, and he reminded himself this wasn't Redstone, where everyone was used to his ways, and put up with them because he got the job done and made theirs easier. Out here, it just made people uncomfortable.

Except Larry. St. John could feel the older man's gaze on him. He wasn't sure what the man was feeling, but it wasn't discomfort.

And not your problem, he told himself.

"What," Jessa was asking, "won't cut it?"

"Signs. Not a campaign."

She frowned. "I know that. I'm just getting started."

She had no trouble, he noted, following him. But then, she'd always been smart. Smart, quick, clever. And wise. Far beyond her years. Of all things, he remembered that.

"Start right," he said.

"Who are you, one of those Machiavellian men-behind-the-throne types? Because as a speech writer, you'd be a failure."

He had, on occasion, been called exactly that: Machiavellian. But not a flicker of the faint jab of amusement he felt—a novelty in itself—made it to the surface.

And then Larry moved, as if he'd come to a decision. He spoke to Jessa, but never took his eyes off St. John.

"I'll be about my business, honey."

St. John, who in turn heard Larry, but never shifted his gaze from Jessa, saw her nod. Easily. Whatever she was feeling, she wasn't afraid of him. He registered the thought with some interest; half of Redstone was afraid of him. He knew that, knew he was part of the Redstone legend, and that speculation was rampant about everything from how and when he and Josh had met to why he was the way he was. He even knew about the betting pool they'd once run. Only the bravest had dared enter, since the goal was to make him laugh.

No one had. So he'd declared himself the winner, claimed the pot, and Josh's pet flight-school scholarship project had gotten a little richer.

Of course, Jessa didn't know who he was, didn't know that

a lot of very smart people walked warily around him. Didn't know that she should do the same.

And didn't know she'd just come closer to making him at least chuckle than anyone had in a very long time.

"I'll check in on your mother on my way," Larry added.

"Thanks, Uncle Larry. She's had a tough week."

St. John remembered Naomi Hill. Remembered her kindness to him, her gentleness. Remembered how she had adored her husband and her daughter, yet quietly kept them both on the right path. It had been his first realization that gentleness didn't necessarily equal weakness, a revelation that had only cast his own mother in a sadder light.

He knew, intellectually, that she must still be deep in grief, and he was more than a little surprised when he felt a flicker of physical response to the thought; his chest seemed to tighten a little. *Odd,* he thought. That didn't happen. It must be the damned memories; she'd been nice to him when most would have ordered the dark, sullen kid he'd been to stay away from their precious, sunny, innocent daughter.

Larry was still watching him as reached the office doorway. "Complete sentences are often overrated, but sometimes useful," he said as he passed him.

No, it wouldn't be smart to take Larry Hill too lightly, St. John told himself. For all his eccentricities, the man was perceptive. As was his niece.

Larry's words echoed in his head as he watched the older man leave through a back exit and, St. John guessed, head toward the big, old house across the storage and parking area for the store. For an instant he wondered what it must be like, to live on alone in the house you'd shared for decades with one person.

He yanked his mind back to the matter at hand, wondering why his usually laser focus was faltering.

He could talk in actual sentences, he thought. It couldn't be any tougher than remembering to speak in another language.

But he wasn't here to make people comfortable. He was here to stop a fiend in his tracks.

"Want to be mayor or not?"

Jessa studied him for a moment before answering levelly, and almost as bluntly, "Frankly, no."

St. John managed to keep from lifting a brow at her, but his gaze narrowed.

"What I want," Jessa said determinedly, "is to stop a man I don't…trust."

St. John felt a knot deep in his gut, both at her hesitation, and at the word she finally chose. He'd done enough research to know that trust was Albert Alden's primary commodity here in Cedar. His facade of upstanding, pillar of the community was carefully constructed and practically unassailable.

"Why?"

The word was out before he could stop it, and it startled him. He never spoke unthinkingly, never let things slip out helplessly. Never.

But Jessa Hill always had been able to get him to talk. When he would talk to no one else, when the simplest of questions seemed dangerous to him, the little slip of a girl he'd first met that day by the river that would eventually be his salvation had always managed to get him to open up. Sometimes about things he'd never spoken of to anyone, before or since.

"Who are you?" she asked, her tone and expression indicating that she thought she was a bit late with the question.

"St. John," he said, knowing a name wasn't what she really wanted. She wanted to know why he, an apparent total stranger, gave a damn about a small-town election.

He didn't have an answer prepared for that. And that realization shook him. He, St. John, the master of planning, thinking ahead and anticipating problems hadn't planned for this simple thing. Had he gotten lax, too far removed from the days when that kind of thinking was the only thing that could save him?

As soon as he thought it, he knew that wasn't true. He did that kind of thinking every day. It was what made him useful—invaluable, Josh said—at Redstone.

Which left him with a conclusion he didn't care for.

"Is there a first name that goes with that?" she asked.

"No."

She lifted a brow and waited silently.

"Not one I use," he muttered, with more effort than he cared to admit.

"Okay, Mr. No-first-name-I-use St. John, I repeat, who are you? And why do you care who's mayor of Cedar? We're only a blip on our own county's radar, and not even that beyond."

"Reasons," he said.

"I can't afford a…consultant, or whatever it is you are."

"No charge." He saw suspicion flood her eyes. "Until it's won," he added. He'd have to figure that out later, he thought.

"And if I lose?"

"No charge."

"How do I know you're not just some plant working for Alden?" she asked, showing more patience with his clipped answers than most outside Redstone.

She had always been that, he thought, *patient.* But, as with her mother, not weak. He'd never forget the first time he'd glimpsed her fierceness, when he'd shown up at the place they met, the little clearing at the bend of the river, sporting new bruises. She'd been beyond upset, she'd been furious, and quite ready to fight for him. He'd never admitted to her who was responsible, although he knew she'd suspected even then. A reasonable suspicion, since it was common knowledge his mother didn't have the courage to swat a fly.

But she'd found the courage to end it….

He shoved back the thought. He was furious with himself. He should have thought of this, should have had a believable answer ready.

"Don't," he finally answered. "But listen. And win."

* * *

This guy, Jessa thought, *has more energy than I ever thought of having.* And smarts, as her father used to say.

Although she'd never gotten a satisfactory answer to…well, to most of her questions, there was no denying this guy knew his stuff. In the hour and a half they'd spent here in the office, he'd come up with more ideas than she had in the week since she'd reluctantly joined this circus.

Using online ads targeted at Internet-savvy residents, and print ads in the weekly community newspaper for those who preferred that medium, she would likely have gotten to on her own. But offering an interview to the radio station in neighboring River Mill, the bigger town twenty miles up the road, wouldn't have occurred to her. The station drew a large audience from Cedar, and an interview for free was much better than paying for a ton of ad time. Nor would sponsoring the local high school's academic decathlon team's trip to the state championships have occurred to her, or providing a special trophy cup at the county fair rodeo competition, in her own favored event of barrel racing.

Neither, he pointed out in that sometimes tricky to follow, extremely abbreviated way, could be put down solely to her campaigning; she'd been involved in both the decathlon and the rodeo during her schooldays in Cedar.

"And just how did you know that?" she had asked.

"Homework," he said.

Meaning he'd done his, she'd quickly figured out. Which brought her back to that same old question: Why? But she didn't ask again, already knowing she'd get the same, nearly useless answer.

She was looking at the back of the envelope that sat propped up against the equipment catalog on the table she'd cleared for them to work on. Clearing the desk in here was not an option. She was so behind already, after just a week of this silly campaign stuff, she didn't know how she was going to manage both and still keep an eye on her mom. Thank goodness Uncle Larry was stepping in more there.

The logo St. John had come up with, in about twenty seconds and a few quick strokes with a pen, was striking and effective. And she had to admit the slogan he'd added, about keeping Cedar in good hands, had a lot more punch than simply "vote for me" in its various incarnations.

"What is it that you do, when you're not meddling in small-town mayoral campaigns?"

"I…facilitate."

"I'll bet," she said wryly, thinking it sounded vaguely nefarious. Not that she had anything against that if it would beat Alden. And obviously, he was very good at it. But she wondered just who he facilitated for. Wondered if she should be more worried about that than she was. Wondered if she was foolish enough to let the fact that she was strangely fascinated by this man cloud her judgment. Wondered if—

"—that picture."

Yanked out of her thoughts, she looked up to see he was gesturing at the framed photograph on the opposite wall, behind what had been—and in her mind still was—her father's desk. She didn't remember the day it was taken—she'd been barely five—but it was unmistakably herself. Her then long, blond hair was held back with a headband, as she looked up with utter adoration at the man who held her hand as they stood in front of Stanton's Café on Broadway, a grand name for the two-lane main road of Cedar, which was even less grand than those twenty-five years ago.

As always, the image of her father, so tall and strong in that picture, made her throat tighten and her eyes brim.

"Connection. Use it."

She blinked rapidly, then, as the sense of what he was saying got through to her, she turned to look at him.

"What?"

"Flyer. That picture."

They'd been talking about a campaign flyer, and what form

it should take. Or rather, she'd been talking, he'd been mostly saying yes or no.

"I won't use my father," she said, getting to her feet and beginning to pace again, as she had several times since they'd begun this. Something about this man made her edgy, almost nervous, a feeling she wasn't used to. And when he touched her, either inadvertently or with intent, to point something out to her, the feeling got worse.

Much worse.

"Not use. Remind."

"They all know who my father is. Was. They don't need a picture to remind them."

"Thousand words," he said.

She nearly laughed. As it was, she turned to look at him, barely able not to grin. "And just what," she asked, "would you know about a thousand words?"

For the barest instant, the corners of his mouth twitched. Whether, had he allowed it, it would have become a smile or a grimace, she wasn't sure. But she'd gotten to him, that she was sure of. And the knowledge sent a jolt of triumph through her that she didn't quite understand.

"Silly not to," was all he said.

"Manipulative to," she shot back, mimicking his mode of speech.

"Politics," he said, paring it down to the essential. And she couldn't argue with that; what was politics, except manipulation? At least, the way Alden and others of his ilk practiced it, even on a small-town level.

"My father didn't," she said as she came back from the doorway to the table. "He just talked to people, they knew him, knew he had their best interests at heart."

"Good intentions."

"And the road to hell, yes, I know. And so did my father."

She walked over to his desk, looked at the big calendar that served as a blotter. It still sat on January, the month he'd died, still had some of the scrawled notes that were sometimes the only record of verbal agreements for purchases. That was all you needed with Jess Hill. And the people of Cedar knew it. They trusted him. Enough to elect him to a record six consecutive terms.

In the beginning she'd told herself she needed those notes— not all the transactions had been completed. But she knew now she just couldn't bear to remove those scribblings in his familiar, loved scrawl.

"He didn't just intend," she said softly, "he did. He got results."

"Yes. You, too."

"If I win."

"Use the picture."

Exasperated, she turned sharply to face him. "And just how would that make me any different than Alden, playing on the death of his first wife and his son, going for the sympathy vote?"

He seemed to go very still for a moment.

"It's enough to make me sick, the thought of him in my dad's place," she said, meaning it. "Not just that, the sympathy ploy, but all this 'welfare of the children' stuff, when in truth he—"

She broke off suddenly, realizing she'd very nearly gone way too far with this man who, despite the intensity of the last ninety minutes, was still a stranger. It didn't matter that, despite his cryptic manner, she felt oddly comfortable with him; he was still a stranger, and she had no business mouthing off about her unproven and at this late date unprovable suspicions.

"What truth?"

His voice was soft, quiet, but there was an edge beneath it that made her even more wary.

"Nothing I can prove. Not against a man everyone thinks is a paragon."

"Not everyone. You."

"I'm a minority of one."

"And who recruited you?"

She shrugged, anxious to leave the subject behind. "Okay, maybe a half dozen who aren't under his spell. But it's still a solid brick wall."

"Use the picture."

"No."

"He's the reason."

"That I'm doing this? Yes. No one would ever have even approached me to run, if not for my father. But I'm still not going to use him. Or his…death, to try and gain some kind of advantage. I just won't."

She was aware she was saying too much again. There was something about that annoyingly terse way of speaking that made you feel you needed to make up for his lack of words with too many of your own.

It suddenly occurred to her that could be a very useful tool. And one he no doubt used to his advantage.

"A factor."

"I know. Some people will vote for me for that reason alone. But I won't use it. I made that clear to the ones who asked me to run. Told them they should find someone else, if that's what they wanted."

"If they had," he said. It wasn't a question by inflection, but she knew it in fact was.

"I'd still be working against Alden. As hard as I am now."

For a long moment he said nothing. And then, slowly, he nodded. "You would."

Again it wasn't a question, only this time it sounded more like a benediction. And that warmed her in a way that was absurd, given she barely knew the man.

It was a feeling she savored even as she worried about it.

Chapter 5

It was worth the twenty-mile drive, St. John thought, to not be staying in Cedar. Although he hadn't liked it much when he'd realized what he was feeling at the discovery that the one inn Cedar boasted was closed for renovations was relief. He'd been so damn sure, so positive that nothing could touch him here anymore, that those demons were long slain, never to rise again. He didn't like thinking he'd been wrong.

He walked across the surprisingly spacious room he'd rented. From the road the place hadn't looked like much, just an older, well-kept motel with fewer than a dozen rooms. But the room was large, with furniture actually made of wood, not some veneered wood by-product, a comfortable seating area and a desk beside the unexpectedly large window with the even more unexpected view.

But St. John wasn't looking at the view. He knew the sweepingly wide and long territorial expanse, with a glimpse of the river through the thick trees, would be beautiful to most, but to him the river was only a jabbing reminder.

He was looking at the screen of the laptop that was open

on the desk. The place didn't run to a wireless connection, or even broadband; that nicety of civilization hadn't made it to this largely rural area yet.

Fortunately he had at his disposal one of Redstone's resident geniuses' handy devices. Ian Gamble's encrypted adapter for his unique cell phone made it possible to use it as a modem with total confidence. It also gave him access to every part of the Redstone network, and, with a few keystrokes, his own personal system in his office.

It made the research brought on by what Jessa had said quick and easy.

Alden, playing on the death of his first wife...

His *first* wife.

For all his talk about doing his homework, he'd failed miserably. He'd been in such a hurry to stop this abomination that he'd jumped the gun. Several guns. He, who prided himself on always being three steps ahead, who anticipated every possibility, hadn't just fallen down on that job, he'd taken a nosedive.

And here of all places—here where he'd first realized that knowledge and preparation and prescience was safety, and that lack of it brought terror and pain—he should have been completely prepared.

But he wasn't. Which brought him back to the irksome realization that perhaps he hadn't vanquished those old demons as thoroughly as he thought he had.

Good thing you brought the laptop, he thought, still angry at himself, *so you can do what you should have done before you ever left Redstone.*

For shorter jobs, he usually relied on the efficient phone's browsing capabilities, but he'd had no idea how long this would take, so he'd packed up the equally efficient and also customized laptop that was now showing him what he should have known long ago.

Of course, knowing this evil as he did, he couldn't imagine Alden would find another woman to marry him. But he saw how ridiculous that was now; of course he had. To the outside world he was charming, polished, the most upstanding of citizens. Women had always fawned over him, a fact he'd never failed to rub in his wife's face to remind her of her own shortcomings.

St. John remembered once when he'd been about nine, overhearing his mother beg his father to divorce her. He would never forget the sound of the laugh that had burst from the man. It had sent shivers down his spine.

"You'd like that, wouldn't you?" his father had sneered. "Get your hands on my money, so you and your brat can live high?"

"He's your son." The protest had been feeble. Only later had St. John appreciated the courage even that much had taken.

"I won't let you embarrass me in front of the whole town. They would never believe you, of course, but I don't want them knowing what a stupid, crazy, inadequate woman I had the misfortune to marry."

"I don't want your money," she'd said with a whimper, so belatedly responding to the original words that St. John, hiding in the crawl space beneath the house where he often hid to avoid his father's wrath, wondered if she really was stupid, or at least very slow. "Just let us go."

The laugh, that hideous, stomach-roiling laugh, came again. "The only way you'll leave is in a box," he promised her. "And I'll have a use for that boy, someday soon."

He hadn't understood, at nine, the box reference. And in his innocent ignorance, he'd dared to hope his father truly might look at him differently, someday soon, when he'd said he'd have a use for him.

"Damn you!"

The words burst from him as a nausea he hadn't felt in years churned up his gut at the memory of just what that use had been. And he wasn't sure if the curse was aimed at his father or himself.

He went back to the screen, this time making himself read the entire piece that was dated three years ago.

How like the man, he thought, to turn what should be a private, personal celebration into a carnival. The wedding had been held in the public square, and the entire town had been invited. And many had apparently shown up, possibly, he thought sourly, as much for the elaborate catered banquet as anything else.

He wondered if any of them thought the ostentatious show in poor taste at the time. Or perhaps now, looking back, the cynical might think he'd done it to put himself in the public consciousness, already with an eye toward challenging the mayor in the next election. That it had come sooner than expected, with the death of Jesse Hill, would have just been a bonus.

He interrupted his reading to look again at the photograph; the woman was attractive enough—his father would settle for nothing less—and not particularly cowed or timid-looking. But perhaps that was how it started, perhaps the rest only came later, when she was so thoroughly broken and trapped there was no escape.

When had she discovered she had married, not the smooth, urbane, amiable man of her dreams, but a monster? Did she even know yet? Could Albert Alden keep his true nature hidden for so long?

He went back to the article, his mouth twisting into a grimace at the near gushing tone of it; the writer had obviously been impressed. Awed, even. The list of notable guests included a couple of county officials, even a local congressman. And, of course, the mayor and his wife. Jessa's father and mother.

The list did not, however, include Jessa herself. An unlikely oversight in the exhaustively thorough article? Or had she purposefully not gone?

Had she even been around?

As often as he'd thought about her, the one memory he

allowed himself from that time, he'd never checked on her. He'd never turned the prodigious network he'd built on her, never tried to trace or track her. He'd told himself he wanted the one, single, bright spot of that dark time to remain untarnished.

But even now, after he'd wondered if she was still here, he hadn't done the research to find out what she'd done in the intervening years. He wasn't certain why he was so reluctant, when the information might well be pertinent to why he was here. He was even more uncertain why he knew this reluctance was different than simply dodging old demons, which was, if humiliating, at least understandable.

He had no idea why he didn't want to probe into Jessa's life. Unless he was afraid of what he'd find. Which made no sense, either.

An image flashed through his head of that odd moment in the office when Jessa had looked at him so intently, her brows slightly furrowed, staring into his eyes as if she were searching for something.

As if she were searching for something she thought she should find.

Something familiar.

He'd stopped breathing for a moment, wondering if somehow, some way, she had recognized him. And his heart gave a ridiculous leap, as if impossibly in hope. He'd sneered at himself the instant he'd recognize the long-lost emotion; he didn't indulge in hope. It accomplished nothing, helped nothing, saved nothing.

But the moment had passed. She had seemed to shake off whatever feeling had gripped her and moved on.

And he'd had to fight down the urge to tell her.

He swore under his breath again. Focus was his best skill, along with compartmentalization. Yet he seemed to have lost his grip on both. Compartment doors seemed to be springing open, and his brain was reeling under the impact of the chaos.

He quickly turned back to scan the rest of the report on the "wedding of the century," a piece of hyperbole that nearly made him gag.

And near the end of the glowing report, he did gag. Because he saw a single thing that made too much too clear.

Also in attendance was the bride's seven-year-old son, Tyler.

Seven. Three years ago. Ten now.

His stomach clenched violently.

The demons broke lose.

His father had a new target.

Chapter 6

"We're small, but we can grow," Albert Alden trumpeted from the gazebo in the town square to the gathered faithful. "We can move ahead, leave the stubborn old ways behind, and prosper. We can make life better for everyone in Cedar."

Listening from the back of the crowd, Jessa was thinking inevitably of her father. Her father had understood Cedar and its people. Had understood the stock from which they'd descended—hardworking, independent sorts, determined to make their own way. He'd been one of them. Stubborn? Perhaps they were. But as her father had been fond of saying, sometimes pure, cussed stubbornness was all that got you through.

A slight movement from the side of the small stage drew her attention; Tyler Alden was restless. The ten-year-old was dressed up in a suit and tie that looked suspiciously like a replica of his adoptive father's, and Jessa couldn't help thinking that a father who dressed his son like himself was slightly odder than a mother who did the same with a daughter. She wondered if she was being sexist about it. Or just suspicious of everything Alden did, from the similar attire to adopting his stepson in the first place, an act that had earned him kudos from most of the town.

The speech went on, and she noted that in typical Alden fashion, the man was making some rather grand statements without much planning to back them up. He was full of big ideas, but could never be pinned down as to how he would carry them out. Yes, a big, modern hospital would be nice, but Cedar hardly had the population to support it, without huge taxes no one could pay and survive. Expanding the smaller, existing clinic, perhaps, she thought. And a brand-new, state-of-the-art library was a pipe dream, the tax base simply wouldn't, couldn't support it. A remodel of the still solid old building, including computer stations, could be done for a third as much. For every big idea he expounded on, there was a cheaper, more practical alternative. Alternatives her father would have begun with.

But then, her father had never been in it for the big impression. He'd been in it because he loved Cedar, and wanted it to be what the people who lived here, people he liked and respected, wanted it to be.

Albert Alden wanted it to be what he wanted it to be.

And the rest of you better just get on board, she thought as she listened.

And many had. Including the *Cedar Report,* the town newspaper that came out three days a week. Although they had always in the past supported her father, they'd recently printed a ringing endorsement of Alden. It had stung, she had to admit that, but she'd been almost glad to see her mother's outrage, the first strong emotion outside her grief that Jessa had seen from her in this eight months of hell.

As was his wont, the longer Alden's speech—she couldn't help the fact that the word *sermon* popped into her head—went, the more dramatic he became. She wondered if he studied video of famous speeches; some of the gestures and phrasing seemed familiar.

Abruptly, she'd had enough. Since it seemed almost everybody in town was here, she should go back to the store and take advantage of the lull to catch up on the paperwork that always threatened to get out of control. And she had some bills to pay. It was going to be tight this month, but they'd make it. Not that she wasn't still worried; her own situation was bleaker. This campaign thing was eating up her savings at an alarming rate.

Dad always told you that doing the right thing sometimes has a price, she reminded herself as she turned to go.

At least at the back of the crowd no one would notice her departure. She had the sinking feeling, as they all seemed enraptured by the man in the covered gazebo, that she could leave the race and nobody would notice that, either.

Maybe she should. She certainly didn't want this, after all. Just because her father had been the longest-serving mayor in the 130-year history of Cedar, and his father the second longest, didn't automatically qualify her for the job.

But if there was anything her father had taught her, in both words and his own actions, it was that not even trying because you might lose wasn't an option.

Something caught her eye as she worked her way along the edge of the crowd that had spilled out into the street. A man standing apart, his hands fisted into the pockets of his jacket as he stared at the man orating some fifty feet away, his expression the most intensely fierce she'd ever seen.

St. John.

As she passed behind him, although she should have been out of his field of vision, he seemed to notice her movement and glanced her way. And that quickly, the fierceness was gone, nothing remaining but the cool calm she'd noticed yesterday. It was so swift and complete that it stopped her in her tracks, and left her with the impression of a man who had changed masks, a disturbing thought, and one she guessed she would do well to remember.

"Deserting?"

His voice matched his current expression. But she knew she hadn't been wrong about the intensity; there had been more than just campaign zeal there.

"I can get his talking points from that flashy Web site of his."

"Half can't," he said, his slight gesture managing to include the throng.

She was surprised he realized that. Most people from big cities were so used to their conveniences, with high-speed wireless even at their local coffee vendor, that the idea of a little place like Cedar, which barely had high-speed dial-up, never occurred to them.

"You'd think he'd realize that," she said.

"Image."

"Hard to create one if people can't access the site."

"Future."

She blinked. "You think he's…building for the future, that Cedar is just a stepping stone." It wasn't really a question, since this had occurred to her early on, when she saw the way Alden was running his campaign, but she hadn't expected this outsider to see it.

Something flickered in his eyes then, something oddly like approval. And again she felt that tiny burst of warmth, and wondered how on earth she'd given this man the power to make her happier with just a look. She reminded herself of that startling change of masks and quashed that pleased sensation sternly.

"I'm going back to work," she said, and started to walk. Without a word St. John turned and accompanied her. That hadn't really been in her plan, but she didn't quite know how to stop him. She felt the slightest of pressures at the small of her back as they worked through the crowd, and tried to ignore the sensation that rippled through her.

He didn't speak—hardly a surprise, given his excessive terseness in general—and even though she'd realized he probably got people absolutely babbling with that trick, she couldn't help but say something. Anything.

"Where are you staying? The Cedar Inn is closed for renovations, and it's the only place in town."

"River Mill."

"The Timberland?"

He nodded.

"That's a drive."

He shrugged. Wordlessly, of course.

A cheer went up from behind them as the crowd reacted to Alden's latest promise.

"This is the second time he's filled the square to over-flowing," she muttered as they had to cross the street to get a clear path to walk.

He still said nothing, but flicked her a sideways glance she interpreted as inquiry.

"He got married there, three years ago. Invited the whole town. And I swear they all showed up."

"You?"

"No. I was in Seattle. Not that I would have gone any-way."

She heard how sour she sounded, and reminded herself to watch that. Openly showing her dislike of her opponent didn't seem like a good idea. Fortunately, he didn't comment.

"College?" he said instead.

"University of Washington," she said as they reached the corner across from the store. "But I was done by then. Had a great job with a veterinary supply firm up there."

"But left."

"Dad needed me," she said simply.

She headed down the side of the store. She wanted to go in the back, leaving the customer entrance closed. Not that anybody was likely to desert the great orator for a sack of feed, she thought.

"Sorry?"

She dug in her pocket for her keys as she tried to work out

exactly what he was asking. Finally she just answered both possibilities.

"That I had to leave? Yes. That I did? No."

She pulled open the door and they stepped inside. The back storeroom was cool and dark and rich with the smell of sweet feed.

"Expensive school." The words came as they walked through to the office. She opened that door, reached in and flipped on the light before turning to face him.

"Yes. If not for Dad and the money he started putting away before I was even born, I wouldn't have been able to go to college in the first place. Or I'd still be paying off massive student loans."

"Planning."

"Yes. And love."

He said nothing, but she saw something flicker in his eyes. Something that made her feel an odd sensation down deep, like that niggling feeling she got sometimes early in the morning when she was still half-asleep, and had to ask, "What was it that was bothering me yesterday?"

Another cheer went up from the crowd down in the square. She didn't think her expression changed, but St. John said softly, "You can."

Startled by his perceptiveness, she turned away and walked over to her father's desk. "But do I want to?"

She'd said it in a whisper, almost under her breath, but he seemed to hear it anyway.

"Only one."

She turned then. "If I am the only one who can beat him, then it's just because of my name."

"Whatever works."

"No one should be elected just for that," she insisted, leaning against the front of the desk. "No more than Alden should be elected just because he's rich enough to afford a flashy campaign. It's not like he earned the money himself."

St. John didn't speak—no surprise—but looked at her

steadily, one brow arching upward. He managed to say a lot in very few words, she thought. And again, she felt compelled to elaborate, even if he hadn't asked.

"His grandfather made their money. Logging, paper, transportation. My dad said he was a real entrepreneur. His son apparently had the same knack for business, but he and his wife were killed in a car accident. Dad said it really took the heart out of the old man."

St. John seemed to be listening intently, so she kept going, although she didn't quite understand his interest. Perhaps it was just a matter of knowing all you could about your opponent.

"My mother thinks his grandfather spoiled him, handed him everything he wanted, never made him work for a thing, because he'd lost his parents. Entitlement mentality explains a lot, I guess."

"Not all."

He said it about as quietly as she'd asked if she really wanted to keep going on this seemingly quixotic quest. But she knew she'd heard it. What she didn't know was what he'd meant by it. Did he somehow know about Alden's predilections?

"I knew his son," she said suddenly.

It was a moment before he said, with no inflection at all, "The one who died."

My God, a complete sentence. The shock may be too much.

"Yes," she said, recovering. "The one who—officially— died in a huge storm and flood here, twenty years ago."

He went very still. "Officially?"

She almost wished she hadn't started this. She had no business having this discussion with a near stranger. And yet she kept doing uncharacteristic things around him, as she had since he'd shown up here that day… Was it really only three days ago?

"I don't believe it."

There. It was out. And she didn't think she was imagining a sudden tension in him.

"Why?"

"Like I said, I knew Adam. I knew the kind of relationship he had with his father. How…bad it was."

She heard the faintest echo of that tension in his voice when, after a moment that seemed as if he were almost struggling to pick his words—or word—he spoke again.

"Meaning?"

"I don't think Adam was just swept away in the floodwaters by accident. I think he let it happen. Or even made it happen."

He seemed to breathe again. "His mother."

"Yes, like his mother. She ended her own misery, maybe he did, too."

"Surprised Alden admits that."

He said it thoughtfully, and the near-complete sentence made her wonder if his thoughts were as clipped and staccato as his speech. Or did he think in full sentences, and just pare them to the minimum before speaking? And most curious of all, why? What had made him develop this laconic shorthand?

"You mean because it might make people wonder if he'd driven her to it?"

"Should."

"Yes, it should. But he has the town convinced she had long been mentally ill, and he'd done his noble best to help her, but she was beyond help."

An odd sound broke from him, something that sounded almost like a strangled snort of disgust. Nobility in a politician was an anachronism these days, she thought. Her father and grandfather had been exceptions. But then, they'd never had aspirations beyond Cedar.

She glanced at the award the town had presented her grandfather at his retirement from office, a bronze sculpture of a man at a lectern with a gavel in one hand. Her father had kept it here where he would see it every day, a reminder to follow as best he could in the footsteps left by very large, nearly unfillable shoes.

She turned her attention back to St. John. He wasn't looking at her. He was staring at a photograph on the wall. Not the one he'd wanted to use in the flyer, but one of her at sixteen with her beloved Max, who had carried her to the state championships. Kula, in a rare moment of stillness, was posed at the horse's front feet.

"Nice horse."

That startled her; he seemed all city boy to her, not the type who would know or care about matters equine.

"He's the best," she said, distracted.

"Is?" He sounded surprised.

"He's twenty now. Leading a well-earned life of leisure. Doc Halperin says it wouldn't surprise him if he made twenty-five."

She glanced at the photo herself, her mouth tightening slightly. She resisted the urge to reach out and touch the image of the dog with the goofy grin.

"If only dogs lived as long," she said softly.

"Still sad?"

"Of course I am. I'll always miss Kula. He was a great, great dog. But we have his grandson now. Maui."

St. John glanced around as if to look for the dog.

"He's been with Mom all week," she explained. "He always knows which one of us is doing worse, and attaches himself."

She half expected him to scoff. He seemed like such a hard case sometimes, disdaining the softer emotions.

But he didn't. "Inherited," he said.

She blinked. That *had* been one of Kula's greatest gifts, that innate sensitivity about who was most in need of his gentle, loving presence. He would try to lure the sufferer into play, with a canine sort of wisdom she'd thought brilliant, but failing that he'd settle in for some long-term comforting. And he had rarely failed at that.

She opened her mouth to ask how on earth he'd known, when he cut her off and began talking about a new idea. She had to admit it was a good one; donating her father's vast collection of books to the town library in his name seemed a good tribute, one he would have appreciated. And the stickers he'd suggested be put in each book would keep her father's name and memory alive for every person who checked the books out.

"No fight?" he asked as she slowly nodded.

"This is different than the picture. It's something I'd like to do anyway, something he would want done. And it's not a piece of campaign literature, playing on his passing."

"Save some," he suggested.

"Yes. There are a few I'll want to keep. Personal ones. The book about the revolutionary war that his great-times-I-don't-know-what grandfather is mentioned in. And the copies of *Tom Sawyer* and *Huckleberry Finn* he read to me when I was little. I was reading Huck to him the day he died." She sighed. "It still has the bookmark he always used, with the little clay dog hanging on it, that I made him in third grade."

St. John gave her an odd look then, one she couldn't decipher. And suddenly he had something else to do, leaving in more than a little bit of hurry.

And she found herself staring at that photographic image of a long-ago loyal companion, and wondering how a man knew so much about a dog he'd never known.

Chapter 7

St. John walked along the path that paralleled the river, trying to convince himself he wasn't as shaken as he felt. He stared down at the water, willing himself with all the power and self-discipline he'd acquired since the last night he'd walked here, to get unwanted, uncharacteristic and unproductive emotions under control.

He left the main path, making his way down to the water's edge. The river was normal now. Wider here after passing through the big bend that formed the raised point of land Cedar sat on, it meandered slowly, the greenish-brown color of the water a reflection of the overhanging trees. Someone had chosen wisely when building the town here, above the flood stage of the river, so that little damage was done unless there was a hundred-years storm.

Like there had been twenty years ago.

He reached the spot. Stopped. Sat down on the outcropping where he had sat that night, shivering in the sheeting rain, watching the river swirl around the base of this huge, jutting rock that was normally a good ten feet above the water.

He drew in a deep breath, as if to prove to himself he could. He'd come close to making Jessa's suspicions a reality that night, although it had never been his intent. He'd thought no further than if he left some things here, some clues, they'd think he'd been caught by the rain-swollen river and drowned.

Once the rain had stopped, he'd made his move. He'd shoved his hoard of cash, saved over the last couple of years, supplemented with a stack of bills purloined from his father's cash box, along with the fancy money clip that held them, deep into his front jeans pocket. The old man would know as soon as he opened the thing, but by then, he'd be far, far away.

Then he had taken the few things he wanted out of his school backpack, and dropped it so the rest spilled out, thinking they would assume the missing things had simply been washed away. Not that anybody would notice anything missing, since the things he was taking were so few and so mundane that nobody would even realize they were gone. But they'd been precious to him. The single photograph he had of his grandparents, kept in part because everyone had always said he'd looked just like the grandfather he'd never known, was in his back pocket, wrapped in plastic left over from a sandwich from his school lunch.

Then came the stone he'd found on his twelfth birthday, the one that was shaped amazingly like a horse head. He'd thought it wondrous, and taken it home. But he'd forgotten it for a very long time in the aftermath of what his father had taught him that very day was his function in the family, now that he was old enough to be "interesting." He'd kept it as a reminder not to trust anything good because it would somehow turn on you.

The two most important things came last. His great-grandfather's cap; just looking at it brought back a vivid, shining image of the man who'd worn it so often.

And lastly, most important, came the most unlikely; a keychain fob made of fired clay, in the tiny, slightly lopsided but eminently recognizable shape of Kula. Important, because Jessa had made it for him, as she'd made the bookmark for her father. Important, because she'd explained, with the kind of seriousness only a very smart, achingly kind ten-year-old could maintain, that Kula could comfort the way no human could, unquestioningly, unstintingly, and this way the dog could stay with him always.

And he had, St. John thought. He carried that keychain to this day, although it was put safely away out of sight for now. And in the end, the small talisman had had much more power than the stone. Power, because it reminded him someone had cared. Power, because it had steadied him in the worst times merely by touching it.

Power, because one day he'd quit carrying the horse-shaped stone along with it because he was afraid it might break the little figure. The lopsided dog was more important.

Only later did he see that day as the turning point, the point when he'd decided not to let his father continue to control him as if he were still there. He wasn't much on symbolism, but that one seemed lit up in neon.

And he knew the fact that the dog had come from Jessa had been the most powerful thing about it.

Something leaped in the water, leaving ripples on the surface that was moving gently, almost languidly today. There had been nothing languid about it that night, it had been all rumble and fury and rush as the rain that was still coming upstream poured in even more volume.

And when he'd slipped on the slick edge of the rock, he'd nearly made his plan more than a stratagem. The rap to the side of his head made it spin, and he'd thought, in the moment when the water closed over his head, that instead of a faked accident it was going to be real. He'd wash up downstream eventually, finally beyond his father's reach.

And he didn't really care. It would be over, one way or another. That had been the goal tonight, and if it happened this way instead, so be it.

And then a tree downed by the storm had caught him, blasting what breath he'd been able to hold out of him. The gulp of water he took in sent him into an instinctive paroxysm of coughing, grabbing, scrambling. And without knowing quite how, he was out of the water, clinging to the downed tree, and back to plan A.

It wasn't until he'd managed to work his way to shore that he realized the tree was the big Madrona he and Jessa often sat under.

It seemed another of those symbols he didn't believe in, and he sent the girl one last, silent, aching goodbye before he stood, somewhat shakily after his dunking, and turned his back on Cedar forever.

Or so he'd thought.

"Damn."

He spat out the word, furious at himself for being unable to control the memories flooding him as surely as the river had flooded the town that night. He'd spent years building walls around this part of his life, and he didn't understand why the hell they chose now not to hold. Just because he was here, where it had all happened? Was he that weak, that just being here could destroy better than half a lifetime of putting it behind him?

Muttering another, fiercer curse, he turned and nearly ran back to the rental car. He got in, slamming the driver's door shut with far more force than necessary. He let his head fall back against the headrest and shut his eyes. Gradually the quietness seeped into him.

After a few moments he opened his eyes. And found himself looking at his own reflection in the rearview mirror. Odd, he thought. He'd had this face now longer than he'd had the old one, the face that had made people who'd known him say he looked just like his grandfather.

But it was his great-grandfather he'd known. Known, and wanted to be like. And Clark Alden would never have countenanced him hiding here in the odd cocoon of this car, dodging old memories. No, Pops would have told him to get back in there and face them, that no good came of hiding.

"All the denial in the world never changes what is," he'd told him repeatedly. "Face it, then beat it or walk away if you have to. Because you *will* have to face it, someday."

He'd thought he had.

Clearly he hadn't.

He started the car and headed back into Cedar.

The rally had cleared out, nothing but the seemingly in-evitable debris large groups of people generated left behind. There were perhaps a few more people on the street, but the throng had for the most part departed.

His brow furrowed when he saw the feed store was still closed. She'd said she would reopen after the rally ended.

Even as he thought it, he saw her. She was coming out of the grocery store down the block carrying not bags, but a large bouquet of flowers. And instead of heading back to the store, she got into the big, blue pickup with the store's logo on the door and drove in the other direction. Curious, he followed.

When she turned into the cemetery at the edge of town, he understood. He thought about simply leaving her in peace, to visit her father's too-fresh grave in privacy. But Jesse Hill had always been, if not nice as his wife had been, at least fair with him. He'd never treated him as if he believed some of the wilder stories, stories St. John had only later realized had likely been started by his own father, as excuse for the stern measures he had to take with his incorrigible son.

He should pay his respects, he thought. To one of the few men in his past life who deserved it.

He felt a bit like a voyeur, following her as she made her way between the various headstones, from simple plaques to elaborate, angel-dressed sculptures. For the Hills, he knew, the family resting place had always been a delicate balance between the elaborate tribute the town wanted, starting with her grandfather's memorial, and the simplicity they themselves preferred.

Jessa had discussed it, back then, with all the ease of a child who has no real concept of death, no true understanding of forever.

"Can you imagine, digging up old aunts and uncles, just to move them all into one place? Gross!"

He remembered it so vividly, that innocent distaste, the wrinkling of her nose as she grimaced.

And if I don't get out of here, I'm going to end up here, next to my mother in that gargoyle-infested crypt, waiting for my father to join us for eternity....

Odd, how clearly he remembered exactly what he'd been thinking that day. Mostly, he'd been yelling silently at himself, for lacking the guts to do what he had to do. He'd been preparing for more than a year, yet still he lingered, sometimes more frightened of what he might find out in the world than he was of what he knew he would find at home.

He watched as she knelt beside the grave closest to the gate in the hip-high fence that enclosed the plot, the compromise that had finally been reached, setting the exalted family apart, yet completely lacking the ostentation of the Alden family crypt some sixty feet away. His great-grandfather had stood fast against the thing until the day he died, and had made his wishes so public it was impossible for Albert Alden to go against them; Clark Alden was buried under a simple headstone much like these here, in a spot with a view of the river.

St. John glanced that way, remembered the devastation he'd felt as the one person in his family, the one bastion that had stood between him and his father, had been lowered into the ground.

It was the last time he'd cried. The last time he'd really felt anything beyond a creeping, numbing cold. Because somehow, even that young, he'd instinctively known it would get worse after that, without the sole governor left on his father's actions.

He'd been right.

He shook his head sharply, focusing once more on where he was now. The Hill plot was shaded by a huge cedar tree, and in the summer the rustle of the branches sounded, Jessa had once said fancifully, like the voices of all those who'd gone whispering to you.

She rose much more quickly than he'd expected. He guessed she did this often enough that a long meditative session wasn't necessary.

He noticed as she got up that the flowers hadn't been one big bouquet after all, but two smaller ones. Who else in the Hill plot earned her attention? Her grandfather's memorial here was merely that; at his wish his body lay across the country, buried at Arlington after he'd served his country with no small amount of heroics in two wars.

She left through the gate, and he drew back slightly, behind the low-slung branches of the big cedar. He wasn't exactly sure why, told himself he didn't want to intrude on this private time for her, but at the same time he felt compelled to follow as she began to walk across the well-tended grass.

She paused to gently touch an angel on a child's stone. The action was so like her it tightened the knot already in his chest. He was still dealing with his response when he realized, with no small shock, that she was headed for that white-marble monstrosity with the name *Alden* chiseled in grand letters.

She laid the second bunch of flowers at the base, on the far side, and stood for a moment with her head bowed. It wasn't where his mother's name was etched, that was on this side. The front, of course, was reserved for his father, and if he knew the old man he already had a majestic epitaph composed.

Beyond curious, he walked around, still keeping enough distance so as not to disturb her. But when he saw what was there, he was the one disturbed. An elaborate bronze plaque, with raised, polished letters.

"Adam Albert Alden
Beloved Son
Tragically lost too soon.
A grieving father's heart that never heals."

Sourness rose in his gut as he stared at the words. And at the dates beneath them, separated by a hyphen, the second date the day he'd escaped. The day he now considered his true birthday, the date by which he marked the passage of years. And then it hit him.

Today was his birthday.

The legal one, anyway. He stared at the date on the plaque, wondering if he'd found the reason why he'd been so unsettled, without even realizing.

Son of a bitch, he thought.

He read the words again. Grieving heart. Like hell. The only thing that old man grieved was the loss of convenience. Nice to have your punching bag and sexual plaything all neatly combined in one package that was completely within your control.

"I'm sorry."

The whisper was barely audible, but it snapped him back to the present. His gaze shot to Jessa's face, in time to see her take a quick swipe at her eyes.

"I should have told, no matter what."

She blamed herself? A shudder went through him. She'd wanted to tell her father, had sworn, with all the passion of her ten-year-old innocence, that her father could fix it, could make things right. He'd known better, but had been moved beyond what he'd thought himself still capable of. He wasn't sure what he felt at the realization that even now, nearly twenty-one years after his "death," she still blamed herself, enough to shed tears.

She spun around, as if she couldn't bear it any longer. The quick movement caught him off guard, and he instinctively pulled back into the shadow of the big tree. But the movement caught her eye, and her head snapped around.

She seemed to relax at the sight of someone she knew. Odd, since she could hardly expect a stranger here. But as he gave in to the inevitable and stepped toward her to explain his presence—although he wasn't exactly sure what he was going to say—she went strangely taut again.

"Why here?" he asked with a gesture at the miniature Greek temple, knowing he sounded gruff, but having some vague idea of the best defense being a good offense.

"It's his birthday," she said, not seeming put off by his tone. "Adam's."

"You…commemorate that?"

"No one else will. And it's partly my fault."

"No."

His voice had gone tight, harsh, but she didn't seem to notice. She simply looked at him, steadily, intently, that tension humming through her almost visibly.

And then, suddenly, her entire demeanor changed. Her eyes widened. She took a deep breath. And said, very softly, "Let me tell you about my friend, Adam."

Chapter 8

Jessa had rarely felt so stupid.

How could she not have realized? Yes, his face was very changed from soft adolescence. His jaw—with the scar that hadn't been there before—was wider, and roughened with stubble again today.

But it wasn't just natural maturation, either; the nose that had been broken so many times was straight now, the slight dent below his left eye, where the cheekbone had been broken and hadn't healed right was gone. A couple of the scars she remembered were also gone, which made her wonder all the more about the one that remained, the one he hadn't had the last time she'd seen him.

But it was also the contours of his face that had changed, and she guessed that when he'd had the scars of his childhood repaired, he'd had them change other things, as well, erasing all traces of the past. His voice had the deep, rough timbre of a man, so different from the boy's. And he was taller, more solid, not the skinny, gangly boy he'd been.

But his eyes hadn't changed. They were the same vivid

blue, and while he'd clearly grown better at masking them, the shadows were still there. How many hours had she stared into them, willing him to change his mind and let her tell someone about what he was enduring?

He hadn't given in then. And he obviously had good reason to not want to be recognized here in Cedar now. The very least she could do was honor that. But at the same time she wanted him to know he—or at least Adam—had not been forgotten.

"He was very smart," she said now, continuing her story. The man who now called himself St. John listened silently. Every line of his body as he sat on the stone bench beside her screamed resistance, but he was listening.

She went on in the most even tone she could manage with all these emotions rocketing through her, coupled with the memories of the girlish fantasies she'd once had about the boy he'd been.

"He never got much credit for that, because everybody always focused on his wildness. Or his supposed wildness. I've always thought most of that was made up, so his father had an excuse for the way he…treated him." He gave her a quick sideways glance. "I know some of it was," she added, "because he was with me when some of the things he was accused of happened."

His eyes closed for a moment, and she wondered if the simple fact of someone believing in his innocence could have an effect even all these years later. With an effort, she went on evenly, as if telling a story to someone uninvolved.

"Sometimes he'd go for days with no new bruises. But then he'd turn up with a hideous black eye, or his nose would be broken again, or an arm. I think he had some broken ribs, once, too. He always said he was clumsy, but I knew he wasn't."

He leaned forward, resting his elbows on his knees. He stared down at his hands, as if that were easier than looking at her. Perhaps it was, she thought. She kept going, softly.

"Then he disappeared for a while. He didn't come to school,

didn't come to our meeting place for days. I was so worried. When I finally saw him again, he had changed so much so it was…shocking. I sensed things had gotten worse, so much worse."

He made a sound then, but it never coalesced into words. Not surprising, she thought. She hadn't realized, had been too young, too innocent to even comprehend, until much later. It had only been looking back, years later, with some unwanted but necessary education under her belt, that she had realized this was the time when the abuse had likely become sexual.

"I tried then, harder than I ever had, to get him to let me tell. I was so afraid for him. I promised him my father could help. He didn't believe me."

"Anyone." He didn't look up as he corrected her without giving himself away.

"I suppose he didn't believe anyone. When the people you should be able to trust most betray you, how can you trust anyone else? I don't blame him."

He still kept his eyes on his hands. After a moment of silence, he asked, "Why bother?"

She couldn't follow that leap. "You're going to have to get more specific on that one," she said. "Why bother with what?"

There was the slightest pause before he said flatly, "Him."

"He was my friend," she said simply.

"Older."

"Yes, he was. Almost five years. It didn't matter. He listened to me. He never laughed at me, even if I said things that probably seemed helplessly naive."

"Crazy. Could have hurt you."

"Oh, I know all the stats. I know how many abused kids become abusers themselves. But I also know that not all do. And Adam never would have."

"Don't know."

"Yes, I do. He would have cut himself off from the world

altogether before he'd let himself hurt someone the way he'd been hurt."

His head snapped up. He still didn't look at her, but he was as alert as Maui when he scented a predator.

"Naive?" He echoed her own word in a voice barely above a whisper.

"Maybe. But I don't think so."

"Never know."

She didn't know how to answer that without giving away what she'd realized, and for as long as he clearly wanted it to be a secret, she would keep her knowledge to herself. She owed him that much, for never having had the courage to do what she should have back then.

Let me tell my dad. He'll help.

No one can help.

He can!

No, Jess. Please.

But—

Don't you get it? If you tell, if your dad so much as talks to him…I'm dead. He will kill me.

The exchange came back to her with a vivid intensity that nearly took her breath away. She remembered those last four words, remembered how he was unlike so many kids who tossed them off so glibly when confronted with the potential of parental anger. "My dad'll kill me when he finds out I lost my history book." "My mom'll kill me when she finds out I cut class."

But Adam had stated it flatly, without inflection, as pure, unadulterated fact.

And she had believed him.

In the end, it had been that that had kept her mouth sealed. She'd seen too much, too many bruises, black eyes and broken bones not to believe he meant exactly what he'd said.

If she told, his father would kill him, and it would be her fault.

And for the last twenty years, she'd lived with the grim

knowledge that he was dead anyway, that her silence hadn't saved him. That she knew, deep in her heart, that it had been no accident that he'd been lost in the raging river waters, made no difference. Even through her pain she understood why he'd done it, why he'd had to finally put an end to it.

And only occasionally did she wish she'd told in spite of everything. If Adam was going to die anyway, at least the world would know his father for what he was. It had been an ugly, sometimes agonizing tangle of emotions for her ten-year-old soul to deal with. A tangle that hadn't gotten much easier as she grew up.

And now, sitting a foot away from the man she should have recognized much sooner, her emotions were still in chaos.

Coming back here, St. John thought, had been a huge mistake. He'd expected it to be unsettling, but never, ever would he have expected it would bring him to this.

He wasn't sure if it had been Jessa's words, praising the long-dead Adam Alden, her tone of lingering, wistful loss, or the simple fact that she remembered him so clearly that had done it, but something had, and as a result here he was, walking streets he'd sworn never to tread again, fighting down a maelstrom of emotions unlike anything he'd experienced in twenty years.

And trying to shake the uncanny feeling that was growing within him that in some way, on some level, whatever had drawn two very unlikely childhood companions together still existed.

He knew perfectly well some would have said, had they known about their secret meetings all those years ago, that it was unnatural that a teenage boy was friends with a girl so young. They would have tried to make it something dirty, evil, when in fact it had been the one clean thing in his life, in his world.

He should have been jealous of her, of her happy, normal life. But he wasn't. His time spent with her was the only taste of that kind of life he'd ever had, and he ached for it, longed for it. Once he had even fantasized about it, wondering if something magically happened to his father, if the kindly mayor and his sweet, gentle, wife would take him in.

But fantasy was not something he'd been able to hang on to for long back then.

It was something he never, ever indulged in now.

Not to mention that the thought of Jessa as his sister, even in that kind of scenario, while it might have been comforting then, was decidedly unsettling now.

And that gave rise to a fantasy he was surely not going to indulge in.

Not for you, he reminded himself.

He was going soft, he thought. All those damned Redstone weddings.

Not for you.

And it didn't matter. He was long past caring. And no matter what Jessa said, he wasn't about to assume he would never sink into the twisted madness his father had.

Odd, he thought, that she had more faith in him than he did. But then again, perhaps not. After all, hadn't she always?

Only when he was certain he was steady did he dare to look at her again. She was looking off into the distance, although he wasn't sure at what. The slight breeze had lifted, tousled first her bangs, then the rest of the short, almost shaggy cap of blond hair. Her nose had that same upward tilt at the tip that had made her adorable as a child, and added a youthfulness now that made her seem even younger than the thirty he knew she was.

He ached to reach out and touch her. Just brush his fingers over her cheek, down that delicate yet stubborn jaw, over the full, soft lips. Need surged through him. He was a man, and no stranger to the feeling, but the power of this wave of yearning stunned him. Suddenly desperate for distraction, he did something he never did; he spoke when he didn't want to.

"More than twenty years," he said.

She gave him a sideways glance, and something in the changeable eyes made his heart react oddly. He didn't stop to analyze the reaction as he usually would, he knew the usual rules didn't apply here, not with Jessa.

"So I should forget?" she asked. "Just go on as if he'd never existed? Not likely. He meant too much to me." She looked away in the moment before she added, in a voice barely above a whisper, "He still does."

St. John's breath caught in his throat. Another uncharacteristic reaction he didn't stop to analyze, although this time it was because he didn't want to know why he was so off-kilter.

"Jess," he said, not sure why he'd been overwhelmed with the need to just say her name.

She looked up at him again. "What?"

He shrugged, shaking his head in negation at the same time. There was no way he could explain any of this.

Not even to himself.

It was only later that he realized he'd shortened her name in the old way. And she hadn't even blinked. She'd explained why she didn't like it back then. He had envied her the reason. And he'd liked that she allowed him the nickname she didn't accept from others.

He shook his head. Clearing his mind of memories was not a task he was used to having to do. And even allowing for the fact that some stirring of those images was inevitable, here in this place where every breath he took felt poisoned by that man's presence, it was unsettling.

Almost as unsettling as realizing that, just as she had been all those years ago, Jessa Hill was his only antidote.

Chapter 9

"Jessa's not stupid!"

"I'm not saying she is. I'm asking if she's smart enough."

"She graduated from the University of Washington cum laude, for crying out loud."

"But is she the kind of politically smart we need? Besides, she's not handling her father's death all that well. Some people are strong enough, some aren't."

"Well, really, it's only been a few months."

St. John stirred his coffee, rather more vigorously than was necessary. He'd come into the small café—the place old man Stanton had banned him from years ago—only for the caffeinated drink. He'd ended up sitting in a booth behind two people arguing the upcoming election. Or rather, the candidates.

"I saw Naomi the other day. She's obviously not making much progress, either."

"That's cold of you. You know the Hills were inseparable. She must be just dying inside."

"I not saying I don't feel sorry for her. I'm just saying we need a strong person in that office."

"Naomi isn't running for mayor. And Jessa is strong. She always has been. She took care of her father, now she's taking care of her mom and keeping the store going. She'll do a great job as mayor."

"Like mother, like daughter is all I'm saying. And there's that loony uncle, too, don't forget him."

"Larry's harmless. Even funny. Every family's got one."

The woman who tried to undermine Jessa, in that nasty, vague way that was nearly impossible to fight, had reminded him of someone when he'd first seen her. But it wasn't until the two rose to leave that he realized she looked like Mrs. Wagman, his old history teacher. With a little shock he realized it was probably Missy, her daughter; the intervening years had not been kind, and the rather glamorous blonde he remembered from when she was twenty and the winner of the annual Miss Cedar River contest now had the look of someone much older than forty, and the tight, sour expression of someone whose main hobby was finding fault.

Jessa's defender he didn't recognize at all, although he made note of her appearance; before this was over, they would need to know who their friends were.

Especially, he thought as he took a sip of coffee finally cool enough to drink, if this was the beginning of the kind of campaign he'd expected all along.

It would be just like his father. He would never be content to let the voters simply decide. He wouldn't risk that. Clearing the playing field was more his style. But his father wasn't a fool, he wouldn't be blatant about personal attacks, not when sympathy was naturally with the woman who'd just lost her father, who happened to be their much-beloved mayor of thirty years. But he would plant ideas here and there, masked by a facade of gentle concern. Just enough to sow the seeds of doubt in enough minds to shift the balance.

Just as he had done with his wife, subtly laying the foundation, then building on it, until everyone was whispering about how unstable she was, how unfortunate he was, yet how noble it was that he refused to abandon her despite her delusional behavior.

And how sad it was that he had such a wild, incorrigible, ungrateful son.

Now, as an adult, looking back, it was so easy to see how he'd done it, how it had worked. But then, for years, he'd been convinced they talked that way because it was true. There had to be something inherently bad in him, something awful. The evil his father had first tried to beat out of him, then—

He stopped the train of thought before it could build up any steam. He was getting better at it, he thought. Soon it would be as easy as it once had been. He was out of practice, that was all.

The waitress offered him a refill, and he shook his head. She shrugged and walked away, wearing an expression he remembered, and that he suspected was common to many small-town teenagers, an expression that said "I hate this place, and as soon as I can leave I'm out of here!"

Funny how he'd never thought of escaping Cedar, not like that. He'd thought only of escaping from his father. But he'd known that without him there as a buffer, to take on part of his wrath, his father would kill his mother. He couldn't abandon her to that.

Later, in cool, dispassionate retrospection, he had realized she had abandoned him long before. When he'd realized she'd known what was happening to him, had chosen to deny it. Or worse, ignore it.

And then she'd made her own kind of escape, completing the abandonment, leaving him to the harsh mercies of the man she knew too well. For a long time her son had wanted nothing more than to follow her into that oblivion. Only a golden little girl held him by a thread—but that thread had turned out to be as strong as tensile steel as she repeatedly made the one argument that ever could have worked.

Don't let him win! He may be bigger, but you're smarter.
You don't know him, Jess.

I know you. You can figure a way out. Just don't let him
win.

And in the end, he had. He'd taken his barely acknowledged
desire to follow the path his mother had to end the torture
forever, and turned it into a way out. He'd prepared, considering
idea after idea and discarding them, all the while making what
plans he could, studying maps, bus routes, staring at the names
of faraway places, all of which seemed inviting for the simple
reason that his father wasn't in them.

He took a long drink of coffee, hoping the caffeine jolt
would help him focus. It was starting to irritate him, this
necessity to force something that had been easy habit for so
long.

He glanced at his watch. Jessa would probably be arriving
at the store about now. She didn't open up until nine—unless
a customer had an emergency, something he wouldn't have
thought possible for a feed store had he not known how many
other adjunct items they carried, from first-aid materials to
basic medical supplies for various animal ills—but she was
always there by eight, just as her father had always been.

He finished the coffee, left a five on the table—about a 200
percent tip for the bored teenager who asked him once about
the refill and otherwise left him alone—and headed down the
street he'd once avoided at all costs, weary of the suspicious
glances that followed him every step of the way. Now the
looks he garnered were simply curious, the kind you'd see in
any small town directed at a stranger in their midst.

He felt no anger about those long-ago glances. People were
only reacting to what they'd been told, to the fiction his father
had so elaborately, carefully spun. He had wished then that
some would have seen through it, but he realized later, from
the vantage point of safety, that it was too much to expect, that
his father was too good, too smooth, too polished. So there
had been only Jessa to believe in him.

He'd never been able to repay her for that.

He would now.

The heavy storage barn door suddenly began to move easily, startling her. She looked over her shoulder and saw... St. John, she reminded herself. If that's who he wanted to be, that's who he was. And she could certainly understand why he'd want to leave any trace of this place and the boy he'd been behind.

She only wished she could leave the girl she'd been behind. The girl who had had such childish dreams about the dark, troubled boy she'd befriended. But there was nothing boyish about this man, and nothing childish about the things he made her think about, not anymore.

Not for the first time since her stunned realization, she wondered exactly what he was doing now. "Facilitator" was no longer enough answer for her. He clearly had enough money to come here, to stay. His clothes, while they didn't scream wealth, didn't indicate poverty, either; they were more classic, the kind of thing that wore forever and never went out of style.

Not, she guessed, that the man known as St. John cared much for that.

So much made sense now. Why he was here, why he wanted to help her defeat Albert Alden. His father. The man who had been the instrument of his pain, his confusion, his despair all those years ago.

But how had he even heard about it? Had he somehow been tracking his father's actions? She supposed she couldn't blame him for that, although it made her even more curious about his life now.

"Thank you," she said as she flipped up the chock that held the door open during business hours. The familiar scent, sweet feed mixed with the fresh green of alfalfa hay, rolled out at her, a pleasant constant to this part of her morning.

He made a small, low sound that could have been

"Mmm-hmm," but was more likely just a very male grunt of acknowledgment.

A sudden memory clicked into place. Adam, telling her he talked to her differently than anyone else. She'd thought at the time he meant "differently" in that he talked to her at all. But now she realized he must have meant he literally spoke differently. In complete sentences.

It made sense now, his manner of talking. He'd told her once that he wished he could just become invisible around his father, wished his father just wouldn't see him. It wasn't a huge leap from that to the idea that unheard was unseen.

The thought that this was a holdover from that time, that to this day he spoke this way as part of the legacy of agony his father had left him, made her heart ache, even as it warmed her that she had apparently been the exception, that he had been careful to talk normally to her. Perhaps only to her.

Anger filled her at the thought. And made her more determined than ever that the man with the polished exterior and the heart of a vicious predator would not succeed. And if he did, she told herself as she double-checked the hay bale count, she would shift her focus, dedicate herself to making his tenure as difficult as possible, raising questions at everything he did, fighting him every step of the way.

"Fierce."

She blinked, looked at him, realized he'd been watching her face, which told her her thoughts must have been reflected there. "If that's what it takes," she said, not bothering to tamp down the intensity she'd been feeling.

"Will," he said. "It's started."

"What has?"

"His real campaign. Rumors. Suggestions. Hints."

Her brow furrowed. "What do you— You mean about me?"

He nodded. "Can't be proven. Or easily disproved. Nebulous. Ridiculous. But stick in people's heads."

"Like what?"

He seemed to hesitate, as if he didn't want to repeat whatever he'd heard. Which meant it was likely nasty. It seemed all expectations of civility went out the window when you were dealing with a monster like Alden.

"Not smart enough," he finally said, with obvious reluctance.

Her brows rose. "Really? Interesting, considering this town sent me off to college with a party, for having the highest GPA in our high school's history."

"Remind them," he said.

She sighed. "What else?"

"Weak," he said.

"I feel that way sometimes," she said with a shrug. "Doesn't everyone?" When he didn't answer, her mouth quirked. "Okay, doesn't everyone, present company excluded?"

She saw that twitch at the corners of his mouth, and barely managed to hold back a smile of her own.

"Next?" she asked instead.

"Unstable."

She nearly burst out laughing at that one. "Please. Who's spent more time in stables than me?" He didn't laugh at her awful pun. "Joke, St. John," she said.

"Serious," he countered.

"How can I take that seriously? Me, the most boring, unneurotic person on the planet?"

"People will wonder. Question."

"But they know me," she said in protest.

"They knew…his first wife."

She might not have noticed a fraction of a second's delay in his answer, so slight was it, had she not known what she knew.

His mother.

Memories flooded her. The adults in her life had been careful about talking around her, but like any child she'd heard and understood more than they'd thought.

It's such a pity, Al is such a wonderful man.

I always thought she just was a bit slow, but apparently it's much worse.

It's so honorable of him, to stay with her, take care of her. And with that boy of his always in trouble to worry about, too.

Did you hear? She actually killed herself.

Stupid.

Crazy.

Unstable.

She hadn't been aware of sitting down, yet she apparently had, on top of the shortest stack of feed sacks. So many of those whispered statements had been preceded by the words *Everybody knows....* But had anyone really *known?* Or had those rumors been as unfounded as the ones about Adam?

"My God," she whispered. "He did it to her, didn't he? He destroyed her by innuendo and rumor. Just as he tried to do—"

She cut herself off before the words *with you* escaped.

She looked up at him, towering over her. He was staring down at her, an intensely focused expression on his usually unreadable face. His jaw was tight—she could see the tension beneath the scar.

"You remember."

The words came out sounding compressed, as if he'd tried to hold them back but failed. She couldn't imagine him failing at much, so she picked her answering words carefully.

"Yes. I was young, but...yes. I remember the whispers, the way people talking about her always stopped when there were kids around, the way they looked at her the few times she ventured out."

"Prisoner."

The word jabbed at her painfully, and she lowered her gaze. "I see that now. Then, everyone thought it was her choice, and that it was safer that way since she was..."

Her voice trailed off, pain and regret making it impossible to go on. She'd only been a small child when Marlene Alden had committed suicide, yet now she still felt as if she should have done something.

Just as she felt she should have done something for the son she'd left behind.

"Crazy," he said, finally completing her unfinished sentence. She looked up at him then. The impassive expression was back, as if those moments of intensity, of emotion, had never happened.

"Yes," she said, seeing no point in denying what he obviously knew.

"Next step," he said.

She wasn't quite able to make that verbal leap. Was he talking about their next step, or Alden's? And then it hit her.

"You mean…his next step will be to try to convince people *I'm* crazy?"

"True to form."

She sighed. "You know, if he can convince enough people in this town of that, then I'm not sure I want to be their mayor."

"Stop him," he said.

"I won't play the game his way," she said warningly as she stood up and dusted off her hands. "I won't be part of bringing that kind of dirty politics to Cedar."

"I'll play it."

"I don't know if—"

She broke off suddenly as Maui rounded the corner of the barn, apparently released today from moral-support duty for her mother. The dog came to a halt, staring at the man beside her. She opened her mouth to tell him it was all right, usually a requirement before the big dog would accept any stranger too close to her. But before she could begin the introductions, the golden plume of a tail began to wag. An almost joyous bark escaped. And amazingly, the dog loped the last few feet between them and skidded to a halt at St. John's feet. Then he plopped down in a perfect sit and looked expectantly upward, tongue lolling happily.

The man stared down at the dog. Jessa never looked at Maui, her gaze was fastened on St. John's face. Maui waited. St. John stared. Jessa watched, intently, even though she wasn't even sure what she was looking for.

Until she saw it.

He smiled.

It was the barest, faintest curving of his mouth, and it lasted only a moment, but as he looked at the dog who was the grandson of the dog he'd once called the best kind of friend in the world, he smiled. And in that instant she glimpsed the boy he'd been.

He'd been her secret heartache, the cause of so many hours of anguish, for reasons that were far too adult. But her heart leaped at the sight just the same; there was still a trace of the boy he'd been, there was still some bit of the softer emotions left in him.

And when he reached out to lay a hand on Maui's noble head, she nearly cried.

"It's like he knows you," she whispered. "He's usually more cautious of strange men around me."

"Good," St. John said, sounding gruff enough that she knew he was just ignoring her first words, not that he hadn't heard them. But the dog's reaction had her wondering about things like genetic memory.

Then the dog was on his feet, eyes alight and tail up alertly as he stared toward the street. They turned as one to look, and saw a dark-haired boy peering almost furtively around the corner of the barn, watching the dog avidly.

Jessa's breath caught when she recognized the child. "It's okay, you can come pet him," she said softly, just loud enough for the boy to hear.

For a moment a smile flashed across the boy's face, much as it had across St. John's moments ago, and he took a tentative step forward.

"Tyler, get back here! This instant!"

The woman's shout from up the street made the boy's head

snap around, and Maui barked sharply. But the boy didn't move, and looked back longingly at the dog.

"Don't make me tell your father!"

The boy went very still. Every muscle in his wiry body seemed to go tense. "He's not my father."

The words were muttered under his breath, barely loud enough for them to hear, and certainly not enough for the woman hustling toward them to hear.

The boy glanced in the direction the angry words had come from, then, for the first time, looked at them.

"I hope you beat him," he said to Jessa.

Then he turned and ran.

Jessa stared after him, her emotions a roiling tangle of old and new. She risked a glance at St. John. Realized by his murderous expression that he knew exactly who the boy was. And knew that he had heard the fear beneath the boy's words, a fear that had been echoed in the voice of the woman calling for him.

"I won't just beat him," St. John said, startling her with the fully formed sentence and almost frightening her with the savageness in his voice.

She opened her mouth to speak, but stopped when she realized she'd been about to call him by his birth name. Because it was the boy Albert Alden had brutalized who was speaking now, she knew. And when he added four words, she knew he meant them as ferociously as if the abuse he'd endured had occurred yesterday.

"I will destroy him."

Chapter 10

St. John saw the knot of a half-dozen people gathered in front of the drugstore a few doors down from Hill's. Taller than most of them, Albert Alden stood out. He was shaking hands, smiling widely, nodding, clapping the men on the shoulder, patting the women's hands.

He realized with a jolt that he had taken several steps toward the group. He stopped. Then, recklessly, he began to walk toward them again, his gaze fastened on the target. A couple of the people broke off and left, then a third waved a cheerful goodbye as he came to a halt barely six feet away. Out of reach, but still as close as he'd come since he'd gotten here.

He watched the polished, practiced moves, the facade of down-to-earth genuineness, all the while fighting the memories that face stirred in him. That face, looming over him, haunting him, until he'd learned about the walls and built a solid, impenetrable cell in his mind for this man and all he stood for.

At least, he'd thought it impenetrable. Until he'd come back here.

Albert Alden looked up sharply, as if, like any predator, he'd sensed a threat. His gaze locked on St. John. He studied him for a moment and then, probably because he knew St. John wasn't a resident of Cedar and therefore of no use to him, went back to his glad-handing of potential voters.

St. John turned away, satisfied. He'd been—unaware—holding his breath as he looked his father straight in the eye for the first time. He released that breath now, knowing there hadn't been the faintest flicker of recognition in the shrewd, assessing gaze.

But there would be. Someday. Soon. He would allow himself that before this was over.

He'd earned it.

"And most of this town thinks he's so damned noble, adopting Tyler." Jessa tossed her pen down on the desk in a movement that seemed as disgusted as her tone. "When I think of what that boy must be going through…"

Her voice trailed away. St. John halted his pacing of her small office, wanting more than anything not to talk about this, but knowing it was going to happen anyway.

"Hasn't started yet."

Jessa looked up at him. "But I've seen bruises."

St. John shrugged. "Beatings, yes. But the other…not yet."

She stared at him for a long, silent moment. "How can you be so sure?"

He had the odd feeling she had asked, not because she doubted his assessment, but because she wanted him to admit how he knew.

And that he would never do.

"Too much fight left in him." He turned away to continue his pacing, telling himself he simply needed the movement, not that he couldn't bear seeing the look in her eyes a moment longer. Not that it helped; the next words broke through despite his efforts to squelch them.

"Still time."

"Time?"

"Take him down before it does."

She studied him for a long moment before she said, "You meant what you said after we saw Tyler. You want to destroy him."

She said it calmly, without surprise or dismay.

"Yes." He gave her a sideways look. "Problem?"

"No."

He hadn't expected her to take it so calmly. But then, she didn't know what he meant by destroy, probably thought he meant it figuratively, when in fact he meant it quite literally. When he finished, there would be nothing left of that particular piece of human scum.

But at the least he'd expected some annoyance that he hadn't come here to help her win, but to make sure Alden lost. Of course, when he'd come here, he hadn't known she was the bastard's opponent.

"I've always known this was about him for you."

Her quiet words shocked him out of his thoughts. It was as if she'd read his mind, had somehow followed those thoughts. His gaze shot to her face.

But then, Jessa had always been able to do that before, and his cryptic speech pattern didn't seem to hinder her much now.

"Mind?"

"Not if you can do what you say. For me, it's never been about winning this, it's been about stopping him."

"I can."

Again she studied him. And again he caught himself wondering if somehow, some way, she was able to see past the physical changes that made him unrecognizable as the boy who had fled this town all those years ago.

"I believe you," she said at last.

For an instant, a brief flash of time, she was that child again, and he was that scared, aching, confused kid, clinging to the one person in his life who had ever said that to him when it mattered. The one person in Cedar who had believed him over his father's accusations.

The person who had followed that fervent declaration with one even more burning, adding one tiny word that made him feel like doing what he'd refused to do in the face of his father's brutality. Cry.

"I believe *in* you."

She'd said it fiercely, passionately, and he'd known she meant it with all the strength of her gentle heart and bright, quick mind.

An urge nearly swamped him, the urge to tell her everything, what he'd done, what he'd become, who he was now. To show her she'd been right to believe in him, to believe he could find a way out, make a life for himself.

A rapping on the outer door reminded Jessa that she hadn't yet unlocked it for business. She moved quickly, letting in a red-haired man in worn denim pants and shirt.

"Hello, Doc. I've got your order ready in back."

"Thanks, Jessa. I knew you would."

"I had to change suppliers, that's why the delay."

The vet lifted his grubby baseball cap, smoothed a hand over what was left of his hair and settled the cap back down before he answered.

"It's all right, we got by."

"Thanks, Doc."

"I haven't forgotten how your father carried us through that rough patch back in the day. I'm not about to shift my loyalty now, no matter what Bracken's does."

St. John watched as she processed the sale of what was apparently some special kind of salt block. Another customer arrived before she finished, a woman in a pair of stained coveralls that somehow managed to look stylish on her thin frame. She gave St. John a curious glance, but said nothing.

Jessa greeted the woman by name, and the two customers nodded at each other and chatted briefly about their respective families as Jessa finished. Small town, he thought. Everybody knew everything about everyone.

Except the dark side of the man who would be mayor.

The man left, and the woman stepped forward. "I know you're not a garden shop, honey, but those berry plants you special ordered for me last year have done so well, I'd like more for next spring. Thirty, I think. You said you'd have to order early for that many."

"Of course. Anything to keep my supply of Margie's jams and jellies coming," Jessa said with a smile that made the woman laugh.

"That's why I come here," the woman said with a laugh. "Those folks over in River Mill, they don't even remember my name, let alone what I do."

"If they ever tasted what comes out of your kitchen, they would," Jessa said.

The woman gave a pleased laugh. "See? Why would I drive all the way there when I can get such lovely compliments right here at home?"

The woman gave St. John another sideways glance as Jessa made notes on an order form. When she finished, she tore off a copy and handed it to the woman.

"I'll call them right away and reserve them," she said. "And I'll let you know as soon as I find out when they'll be shipped."

"Thanks, Jessa," the woman said. "Give my best to your mom. You're both on my mind every day."

"I will. And thank you. It means a lot."

The woman turned to go, gave St. John one last glance, then looked back at Jessa.

"Sweet. Hope he's more than a customer, honey," she said with a conspiratorial wink. Then she flashed a grin at St. John, a grin that lit up her rather plain face.

The teasing caught him off guard, and he pretended to be

fascinated by the display of birdhouses. But not before he'd noticed that Jessa had blushed. Furiously.

When she had finished with her phone call—when she'd said right away, she'd meant it—she busied herself filing the order in the box beside the register.

"Bracken's?" he asked. "In River Mill?"

She looked at him then. He hadn't been sure she'd been avoiding it, but he was now, by the relief in her eyes at the change of subject from Margie's arch comments.

"The feed and garden store there."

Something in the way she said it made him want to pursue the inquiry. He waited silently as she made a note on another order and refiled it.

When she turned to go back to her office, he realized she wasn't going to elaborate unless he pushed. Unlike most people, Jessa didn't seem always compelled to fill the silence, which made the technique much less effective.

"New?" he asked as he went after her, knowing they hadn't been around when he'd been here.

"Not really." She went to the desk, sat and reached for a stack of folders before continuing. "They opened about six years ago. Never been a problem for us, until they started undercutting our prices by enough to lure people to make the drive."

He went still. "When?"

"A few weeks ago. Everybody in town started getting flyers."

"How bad?"

With a grimace, she looked up from the folder she'd opened. "Bad enough." She tapped a slender finger on the papers in the folder. "I know how much the stuff they're selling costs, and how much it costs to get it out here. I don't know how they do it and stay in business."

I'll bet I do, he thought.

His jaw set, he began to make plans.

Chapter 11

Jessa didn't have to try to keep herself busy, didn't have to look far for distraction. The work was always there waiting, and she never seemed to catch up. If it weren't for her mother, and the fact that she needed to be with her as much as possible right now, she'd have spent all the evenings after they closed here in the office, trying to at least get even on the paperwork.

It wasn't that she didn't want to be with her mother, she did. She was the only person in the world who truly shared her grief, who had been as devastated as she at the loss of the man who had been their rock. But this store was their livelihood, had been her family's for decades, and she couldn't neglect it, either.

She thought again of that conversation with St. John about Bracken's. His intensity had seemed odd for the subject. It wasn't his problem, after all. But while his face had been his usual expressionless mask, his voice had betrayed a laser focus.

Yet after that morning he'd seemingly vanished. She hadn't thought much of it the first day, but after the second ended without a sight of him, she wondered if perhaps he'd changed his mind about this whole thing and gone as unexpectedly as he'd first appeared.

The thought unsettled her. She had things she wanted to ask, to know, not about the election, but about the boy he'd been and how he'd become this mysterious, laconic to a fault man. Perhaps she should have told him she knew who he was the moment she'd become certain. At least then she might have gotten some answers.

The fact that Adam Alden was not just alive, that he hadn't merely survived, but had apparently done well enough to truly make something of himself—although she had no idea what—had been a source of constant joy, wonder and more than a little bewilderment ever since the moment in the cemetery when she'd finally realized what she should have known instantly.

But she wanted to know how he did it, where he'd gone, and she only realized how desperate that desire was now that the chance she might never know was looming over her.

"He'll be back. He wants to beat his father too badly to give up," she told Maui, who was sprawled beside her on the office floor.

She turned her attention back to the paperwork on the desk. She'd come in here to work, not dwell on things she had no control over.

Her mother had gone to bed early, so Jessa had grabbed the chance to do some paperwork. The store was dark, the single desk light in the office and the glow of her laptop screen behind her the only sign that someone was here. She went at the papers methodically, sorting, making notes from each order on the chart she kept on their regular customers. It was something her father had started, and she liked the idea of always knowing what their best customer's preferences were, but she knew there had to be a better way than her father's voluminous handwritten notes barely kept together on a clipboard. She—

"Need to computerize."

She jumped up, her heart slamming in her chest as a shadow loomed over her. She knew in an instant who it was, but oddly, her heart didn't calm. It just seemed to race in a different way, her pulse pounding along too quickly, the heat of that acceleration flooding her as she stared at him.

"Sorry," St. John said.

"You should be," she said, and then, looking down at Maui, added, "And so should you. Some watchdog you are."

The big golden simply looked from her to St. John, that plumed mood-indicator of a tail telling her that the dog was delighted at the late-night visit. And to be fair, as she'd been working she'd noticed, vaguely, that the dog had lifted his head and made a tiny sound moments before, and she could hardly expect him to bark at someone he'd been properly introduced to as a friend.

Or someone his DNA told him was a friend, she thought, laughing inwardly.

Laughing at herself over the dog's reaction, so she didn't have to deal with her own? she wondered.

She looked down at the papers she'd been working with, afraid that he would see her heated cheeks. Because she couldn't deny the truth of that assessment; every time she saw him—or even thought of him—she reacted as if she were that long-ago child, half crazy about him in too many ways to count.

Not that that wasn't perfectly understandable. Once you got past the terseness of his conversation, if you could call it that, the man who called himself St. John was nothing less than a presence. He made most of the men she'd known seem like pale imitations of men, made them seem like they were simply existing while he was vividly, almost violently alive.

Perhaps that's what barely surviving did to you, she thought.

Never mind what he was doing to her.

And never mind the fact that, deep down, she was all too

well aware that there was nothing childlike now about her reaction to him. Nothing childlike about the jump of her pulse, the rush of heat or the quickening of her breath. Even the man she'd been engaged to in college hadn't done this to her.

It was just the shock, she rationalized. The shock of finding out he was alive, after years spent telling herself she was crazy, spending any time longing for someone long dead. Remembering was fine, appropriate, fitting for the boy she'd cared so much about. Mooning after a ghost had been something else, something she'd told herself countless times she should give up.

"Still should."

Her heart slammed again as he seemed to read her innermost thoughts. And then she realized he was looking from the stacks on the desk to her open laptop, and had returned to his original statement about computerizing the store's process.

Get a grip, Hill. With an effort she managed it, and answered evenly enough.

"I'd like to. I just can't find a software program that will do all I want it to."

"What?"

"There are tons that will keep books, or do inventory or track purchases, all that, but I want one that will coordinate all that, tell me where some of our more obscure stock is stored, plus keep track of individual customer preferences and cross-reference them with other data, without having to input everything two or three times. I'd like to be able to let people who buy certain products regularly know if I come across a bargain on those, so they could stock up at a lower price. That kind of thing."

"Good service."

"That was my father's trademark." She sat back down wearily. "But I've been looking for nearly a year, ever since I finally convinced Dad it would be good for business, for a program that would do it all. It doesn't seem to exist."

"Could."

"Should," she said, earning a twitch upward at one corner of his mouth.

"Know someone," he said.

She frowned, working it through. "You know someone who…?"

"Could write it."

She lifted a brow at him, waiting silently.

There was no doubting the near-smile then. And for an instant, just an instant, a glint of humor in his eyes told her that he understood perfectly that she was turning his own methods back on him.

That glint, that flash of amusement, nearly took her breath away.

She'd often wondered, back then, what Adam would be like if he'd had a normal life. Wondered how he survived a life without the simple things she enjoyed: love, happiness, laughter. Somewhere, somehow, he'd learned to laugh, even if he couldn't—or wouldn't—let it show. The thought flooded her with relief; perhaps his life hadn't stayed the crippled, twisted thing it once had been. Perhaps he'd truly managed to have a good life in the years since he'd escaped his father's clutches. It had been twenty years, after all, plenty of time to…

Find someone to help him along that path? He wore no ring, but that meant nothing. On the heels of her earlier acknowledgment of the effect he had on her, the idea was a jolt.

It's been twenty years, she told herself. *Why wouldn't he have found someone, some caring woman who would see the true person he was, who would help him get past the scars, the pain, and find some peace?*

She scrambled to cover what she very much feared had shown too clearly on her face.

"You know a software writer?"

"Good one. Barton. I'll ask." His mouth quirked. "Tear him away from his fiancée."

He looked oddly bemused for a moment. Something about the expression jabbed at her, because it spoke of the life he'd left to come here, and the people in that life. The life she knew nothing about. She wanted to ask where he worked, what he did, what he had been doing since the last day she'd seen him. She wanted to know everything. But she was afraid if she asked too much too fast, he would close up again.

And she couldn't think of a way to do it without betraying that she knew who he was.

She settled for an innocuous question. "You work with computer people?"

"Sometimes," he said. Which could be, she thought wryly, true of almost everyone on the planet.

"They'd be lost here," she said. "Cedar is pretty low-tech."

"He says he'll fix that."

She knew he was no longer talking about his computer person. "Sure. He'll put computer terminals in the library, in the town offices, even the post office. Only problem is that we're still stuck on dial-up. We're too far from the phone company central office to get DSL service, and cable hasn't come out this far yet, so the only alternative is very expensive satellite service, the cost of which he conveniently leaves out of his plan."

He nodded at her, as if she were a student who'd done a good job on her homework. For some reason that irritated her.

"Just because I don't want to be mayor doesn't mean I haven't thought it through."

"Never said that. Just need to tell people."

"They all know that already."

"Listen to dreams enough, forget reality."

She barely managed to refrain from pointing out that that

had never worked for him. But then, his reality had been much, much uglier than most.

Unable to look at him any longer, she turned around as if there was something she needed to check on her laptop screen. Which, she realized, there was.

"That reminds me," she said, more to herself than him, "I need to go online and set up a payment."

She plugged the phone line into the laptop's modem and started the connection process.

"Slow," he said after a minute went by.

She shrugged. "Takes forever, but now I have to do it this way. Can't risk another problem with the bank."

"Problem?"

"A couple of payments got there late even though I mailed them five days in advance and they only had to go to River Mill. And one didn't get there at all. They started making nasty noises. Don't know what's up with the mail, but I don't trust it anymore, not for this anyway."

The connection finally made, she logged on to the bank's home page and waited again for the slow process to complete. He walked closer, looking over her shoulder.

"What bank?"

"River Mill Savings and Loan," she answered as she entered the payment information and sent it. "So far this is working. If it happens again, I'll be hand delivering it, and standing there while they post it. But I can't really afford the time to drive up there and back every month, especially now. Never had a problem in all the years we've dealt with them, but lately..."

"Pattern."

She looked up at him then. "What?"

"Phone calls," he muttered, looking suddenly a million miles away.

Before she could ask what he was thinking, she had to turn back to the screen so she could watch and confirm the transaction had registered. When it did, she saved a copy of the confirmation number. Finally finished, she set her mind to the task of interpreting yet another set of cryptic comments, and turned to look at him.

He was gone.

Chapter 12

St. John paced his motel room, as he had been doing most of the night. He didn't require much sleep—in fact, he tended to look upon it as a waste of time, and the necessity for it annoying. On some level he suspected he was trying to regain all the time he'd lost to fear and cowardice, but he never spent much time anymore analyzing why he was the way he was. He'd found a balance that worked, kept him going, and he was, if not happy, content with that.

At least, he had been, until he'd come here and found himself buffeted on all sides by a past he'd thought too deeply buried to matter.

He paused before the window, although he could only make out vague shapes in the darkness, and there was no moon tonight to glint off the river.

He'd made some calls, some to Redstone people who were used to his oddities and some to people who had been irritated by the nighttime disturbance, until they realized who was calling. The people he dealt with outside Redstone might not always be fine, upstanding citizens, but they always cooperated with him. Of course, he made it worth their while, in one way or another.

Then he'd settled in to wait for the required information to return to him. It shouldn't take long, he thought. He knew what was happening, he just needed confirmation.

And it would come. This was a skill he'd gained after his life with Albert Alden. Assessing what the people you encountered could do for you, if not right now, then down the road. Then it was making sure they either owed you or knew it would be worthwhile if you owed them. And in the years of his young life that he'd spent in the darker, shadow-filled places, before Josh had pulled him back into the light, he'd acquired quite a collection of contacts that served him—and Redstone—well to this day. He could still move in that world if he had to, and sometimes did, since it paid off so well.

He spun away from the glass, wondering why he was standing there. It was this place again, he muttered to himself. He hadn't spent so much time dwelling on who he was or how he'd gotten here in years. It was this damn place making him think too much about such useless drek.

And Jessa.

The little voice in the back of his head refused to be silenced this time.

All right, face it, he ordered himself. *She was the one clean, golden, beautiful thing in your life. The only bright spot amid all the darkness and pain. Did you really expect to face her again and feel nothing?*

The sad answer—sad because he'd been so incredibly wrong—was yes. He had expected just that. He thought he had crushed those old feelings into not just submission, but nonexistence.

Finding out that he hadn't was beyond disconcerting. He was sitting here, aching inside in a way he hadn't felt since the night he'd sat on that rock, watching the ferocious rush of water below him, knowing that this was his one chance, his best chance, and realizing with a matching flood of shame that he was too big a coward to take it.

Jessa.

An image of her slammed into his mind, not from those days, but now, when he'd stood on the corner where he could see the house she'd grown up in, and he'd seen her throwing a tennis ball for the big dog. She'd always had an athlete's grace, and still did. Heedless of the dirt accumulating on the ball the dog tirelessly chased, she kept the game going, cheering when he caught the once yellow ball in midair, and laughing at the animal's limber doubling back on himself when he inadvertently overran the treasured object.

Even now she could laugh. She'd always had that, that sense of joy, of pleasure in life. Something he'd never had. Something he wasn't capable of. He wondered if he would have been, had he grown up as she had.

He walked over and sat on the bed, stretching out his legs and leaning against pillows propped up against the solid wood headboard. Seemingly unable to resist, he let another image unwind in his head, of the night they'd spent mapping out a true campaign, of the moment when he'd stood over her as she sat at the office desk, when he'd caught himself staring down at the slender nape bared by the tousled cap of her hair. Delicate. Vulnerable. Beautiful.

Little Jess, who had been his lifeline, was now disrupting that life in ways he'd never experienced and didn't quite know how to deal with.

When his cell phone rang, it jolted him out of a sleep he hadn't been aware of drifting into. It also interrupted a dream the likes of which he hadn't had since teenage hormones had been running high.

He seized on the call as distraction from the unaccustomed ache of his body. He was as subject to early morning hard-ons as the next guy, but this, this was different. This wasn't just the usual surge, this was specific. This was for Jessa, who had been the vivid, sexy star of that crazy dream. Jessa, the child of his memory, now the woman who haunted him. Because she was definitely that, a woman. All woman.

"St. John," he muttered into the phone, shifting to sit up on the edge of the bed.

"Crankier than usual, are we?"

He blinked. "Josh?"

"I figured you'd be up."

Depends on your definition of up, St. John thought with a grimace.

"Didn't expect you."

"Just called to say my theory has now been proven." Josh's drawl was laced with humor, and St. John braced himself.

"Theory?"

"It takes three people to do what you do, and not nearly as well."

Guilt jabbed at him. He shouldn't have just abandoned Redstone like that, he—

"That was true, but a joke, my friend. Stop feeling guilty about taking some time for yourself for the first time in… nearly forever."

Josh knew him too well, St. John thought ruefully. That's what happened when you let people get close—they could see right through you, to your darkest, most hidden corners. Like Josh.

Like Jessa.

"Can do some from here if—"

"No, we're struggling through," Josh interrupted. "For a change I have some info for you."

"You?"

Josh chuckled. "Without your…more interesting contacts, we had to go through more direct channels to find out what you needed."

Meaning, St. John realized, that Josh had used the considerable weight of the Redstone name and himself to get the info St. John had asked for. He felt worse now; he knew very well that Josh didn't, as a rule, trade on his own prestige and power.

Unless it was for one of his own.

And you're one of his own.

"Mac's wife has some connections in the animal feed industry," Josh was saying.

Emma, St. John thought. Emma McClaren and her Safe Haven animal shelter. Of course she would.

"She made some calls, found out you were right. Alden's been subsidizing the store in River Mill, enabling them to undercut on price."

He'd known he was right, but it was good to have it proven.

"How involved?"

"Apparently the whole idea was his. The advertising, the pricing. The owner needed a loan, couldn't qualify at a bank, and Alden gave him a personal loan with those conditions."

Exactly what he would have expected. Some things never changed, and his old man's techniques definitely qualified. Business or personal, control and coercion was what it was all about.

"Nice way to do business," Josh said. "Can't beat them honestly, on product or service, so set out to destroy them underhandedly."

St. John just stopped himself from pointing out how much of the world did business that way. He knew that Josh knew it. Knew it so well that Redstone had been founded—and had grown into the global force it was—on the opposing principal; hire the best to do the best, and get out of their way and let them do it.

"Seems Alden also has a mole of sorts in that bank. Ryan managed to…get a look at some records."

Guilt jabbed him again. Ryan Barton, one time hacker and now resident Redstone computer genius, had sworn off his more illicit activities when Josh had hired him after he'd hacked Redstone's own system. Unless it was to help one of the Redstone family. And now he'd had to dust off those not so legal skills, and it was his fault.

"One payment was posted then removed," Josh went on, "and reposted after the due date. After that, they were simply posted late. Even the third one, that was sent certified mail, didn't get posted until two days after the post office showed it had been delivered. Somebody could have a legal case there, if they wanted to pursue it."

"Might," St. John muttered.

"And, I don't know if it matters, but did you know Alden has been stashing money in an offshore account in the Caymans?"

He blinked. "What?"

"Mac dug that up."

St. John stood up. What had Josh done, assigned everyone connected to Redstone to dig into this? Harlen McClaren surely had better things to do—like finding another sunken treasure, or making another billion on some clever investment no one else saw the worth in—than poking into this tiny-scale situation.

"He had the connections," Josh said easily. "Apparently it's not a huge amount, but enough to fund a very comfortable retirement. If it's significant to you, I'll put Ryan to work backtracking the deposits."

"I…" For once the monosyllabic response was because he didn't know what to say. "Don't know yet," he finally answered.

"All right. I'll have him keep on it, just in case. In the meantime, Ryan's working on that software you wanted. Should have a beta version in a few days, he said."

"Bill to me."

"Like hell," Josh said.

"Josh—"

"No more about it, Dam."

"Didn't have to mobilize all Redstone," he muttered.

"Are you kidding? They were lining up at my door to find

out what they could do, once they heard it was you asking. You've made every one of their jobs easier at one time or another. So shut up and let them at least feel like they're paying you back a little."

He sank back down on the edge of the bed. He might not talk much, but he was seldom totally speechless. He was now. And his stomach knotted even more when Josh added quietly, "Let *me* feel like I'm paying you back a little."

St. John swallowed. Hard. Fought against betraying the fact that unaccustomed emotions were tumbling through him.

"Backward," he finally muttered.

It was all he could think of to say.

"I don't have it backward. I don't trade on obligation, you know that," Josh said. "Worth for worth. You're an investment that paid off big-time." And then, after a moment's pause, he added, "And you're my friend, Dameron St. John. In case you've forgotten."

"Haven't," St. John said, barely able to get even the single word out.

"And since I know how much you enjoy personal conversations," Josh answered with a laugh, "I'll leave it at that. Let me know what else you need. Let anyone here know. It may take more of us to do your job, but we'll do it."

After Josh had hung up, St. John sat on the edge of the bed, cell phone in hand. Here in this place, just a few miles from the lair of the beast, he'd been forcibly reminded that this was no longer his life. His life was far away, among the people of Redstone, who had become the family he'd never had. Who turned to him when they needed something, and who he, amazingly, could turn to.

A woman who'd thought he needed analyzing had once asked him if he trusted anyone. His first answer—unspoken because he wasn't about to answer someone he already knew he would never see again—had been no. But he'd realized that was far from true; he trusted anyone Redstone.

Jessa would fit there, he thought. Perfectly. She had all the requirements for Redstone; brains, wit, drive, generosity and the kind of loyalty Josh didn't have to demand but earned, given as his rightful due in return for his own loyalty to his people, the loyalty that put Redstone consistently among the top-ranked places to work not just in the country, but in the world.

He had that power behind him, and he could, and would use it to bury the abomination that was his father.

Forever.

Chapter 13

Jessa didn't put up the Closed sign when lunch rolled around. She'd decided she couldn't afford to close. Not that it would make much difference, the town was so used to Hill's being closed from noon to one they probably wouldn't even look or notice.

It meant she couldn't go back to the house and see her mother, but she was doing better this week. Naomi had rallied at the idea that Hill's was in trouble, and had even said she would come in herself; she hadn't worked in the store in years, but surely she could still be of some help.

Jessa felt a bit slow on the uptake; she should have thought to get her mother involved in the store again. Not that her father's absence was any less noticeable here; in fact, in some ways it was more painfully apparent, but there was work to be done, and that was always a good diversion.

She headed back to the office to grab the sandwich she'd brought in. And stopped dead in the doorway when she saw St. John leaning against the edge of the desk, his long, jeans-clad legs stretched out before him, his arms crossed over his chest, simply waiting.

He wore the driving cap he'd had on that first day, although when she stepped in he removed it. She wondered where he'd picked up the manners, since she knew his mother had been too far gone in despair and surrender to have bothered. The cap made her curious; it seemed from another era, dated—at odds with his young face—and yet it suited him. And showed he could care less about current style or the lack of it.

Not that anyone cared much about current style around rural Cedar, where function was king. Anyone except Albert Alden, that is, with his city-tailored suits, silk ties and more silken tongue. Problem was, since they rarely saw the like, a lot of people in Cedar were impressed, even proud that such a polished, articulate, successful man had come from their little town.

"Newspaper," St. John said, gesturing at her desk with a nod.

So much for the niceties, she said. And obviously any explanation of where he'd vanished to last night was out of the question.

She walked past him and looked where he'd indicated, expecting to see a copy of the *Cedar Report*. But there was no newsprint in sight. Instead, there was a text-dense printout that was slightly blurry.

"A fax?" she asked.

"No printer. Fax at the copy store."

"I have one you can use," she said absently as she tried to spot in the document listing various financial interests—she assumed, given his shorthand, that they were the owners of the *Report*—what she was supposed to find. "It's just an inkjet, but—"

She stopped, frowned as a name in a subsection of a subsection caught her eye. "Wait a minute…isn't this Alden's corporation name?"

"One of them."

She looked up at him. "You mean he owns a piece of the newspaper who endorsed him?"

"Big piece," was all he said, but he was giving her that look again, as if she were a student who'd done well. Only this time it pleased rather than irritated her.

"How can he do that?"

"A few layers deep."

"You mean he's hiding his interest?"

"Corporation owned by holding company owned by trust."

"Well," she said in disgust, tossing the paper down on the desk, "that explains all the free propaganda thinly disguised as news articles."

"Not so free."

"No. Looks like he paid handsomely for it."

"More."

"More than handsomely, or there's more?"

"B," he said.

She waited.

"Subsidizing Bracken's."

She leaned back in the desk chair, her frown renewed. That made no sense, what did that have to do with the election?

He went on. "Paying someone in the River Mill bank."

She blinked. "Paying who to do what?"

"Your 'late' payments."

She sat upright abruptly. Then, slowly, she stood, her gaze fastened on his face.

"You're telling me," she said very carefully, "that Albert Alden is trying to sabotage not just me, but Hill's? Why would he do that? To distract me?"

"Partly. But if you can't run a business," he said with a shrug.

She got it then. "Then I can't run a town," she said as the explanation dawned. "Now there's an irony, given he inherited his money."

Something shifted in St. John's face then, pain flickering

for an instant in his eyes. And she remembered the night he'd hesitantly told her that the only person in the world he truly trusted, besides her, was his great-grandfather. The man who'd made the Alden fortune, who had lost his only son tragically young, had lived to see his grandson turn out a twisted wastrel who thought because he didn't have to work he shouldn't. The old man had been the only real support young Adam Alden had had.

She wondered just how much the man had known. He'd died a couple of years before the abuse had become noticeable, she knew that much, but had he suspected? Was that why he'd been so close to his great-grandson, in an effort to protect him? Or had Albert Alden's viciousness only been unleashed upon the death of the one man who had any control over him? Those were answers she needed, answers she had to have, or her heart was going to burst under the painful pressure.

"So he really is trying to buy this election," she said, making herself keep to the subject at hand. "And he's not even doing that cleanly."

"Two years ago bought controlling interest in Riverside Paper."

She sank back down into her chair. Outside of the shopping area her father had shepherded, the paper producer was the biggest employer in the vicinity, and one of the biggest in the county despite the fact that it had been struggling of late, her father had said due to poor management and harsh environmental restrictions. And Alden controlled it?

If she had to guess, she'd bet that of the working people in Cedar, nearly half got their paycheck from Riverside Paper. Which meant they owed their livelihood in part to Albert Alden.

He wouldn't even have to try to scare those people into voting for him. They were already scared, given the state of the company.

"So they'll vote for the man who figuratively signs their paychecks, whether they want to or not," she murmured.

"History proves," he said. Then, amazingly, he added, "Quick learner."

"Me? Hardly. I feel like I'm in way over my head. This was supposed to be a small-town election, not some dirty national-style tangle."

"Springboard."

She grimaced. "You'd think if he was going to do that, he would have started at a higher level, county government or something."

"Influence takes time."

"And he's chosen his path very carefully, hasn't he?" At St. John's nod, she sighed. "Politics…you know, if he'd put half this much energy into honest work—" She stopped, shaking her head ruefully. "Did I really just put politics and honest work in the same sentence?"

He laughed.

Jessa's breath caught in her throat. It had been a short, sharp, rusty sort of sound, but it had been a laugh, and it sent a jolt of pure pleasure through her.

He looked away, as if he'd been caught doing something illicit.

While your father looks people straight in the eyes and lies through his bleached, straightened, perfect teeth, she thought.

"It's time," he said, and she saw he was staring at the photographs on the wall again.

She didn't know what his plan was. And she wasn't sure why she found herself thinking of a snowball starting down a mountain. Or a general before a strike that would change the course of a war.

What she was sure of was that it would happen exactly as he planned.

In his perverted abuse of his own son, Albert Alden had made an implacable enemy.

Chapter 14

What a difference a week made, Jessa thought.

When she'd thought of St. John as a general, she'd had no idea how right she was. With an almost military precision, things began to happen.

That it was St. John's plan she had no doubt.

That it was working, she couldn't deny.

She was awed. Amazed. And feeling more than a little wonder at the speed and meticulousness of an operation that was happening completely behind the scenes, beneath the radar.

But what was in the forefront of her mind, despite all these things, was the ever-growing need to know, to understand, who this man was. And how he'd become a man able to bring incredible influence and pressure to bear in such a short time. How had battered, tortured Adam Alden become this cool-headed, taciturn and undeniably powerful force of nature?

A customer drew her attention, then more of it as she had to search her memory to recall where the sewing machine needles had ended up. She smothered a sigh as she rang up

Mrs. Walker's purchase. She simply couldn't keep up with all the stock they carried and run the store, too. She had hired a local high school student—Mrs. Walker's nephew, in fact—to do the more physical things, like move things from the barn into the store when inventory got low, or put items on shelves. Problem was he sometimes put things away where they would fit, not necessarily where they would go in a logical way.

As the woman left, she realized that computerizing needed to happen sooner rather than later, even if she had to go with two or three programs to accomplish what she wanted. With as much time as she spent finding things and updating things manually, she could input the data, a bit at a time. It would take a while, and for that time she'd be doing double duty, but she could handle that.

She just didn't know if she could handle that and this campaign at the same time. She'd have to—

"Sewing machine needles?"

She nearly jumped. She was getting more used to the silent way he moved, but he still startled her too often for her comfort. She wondered if that stealth mode was something he'd developed as a kid, trying to hide his presence from his father.

"Not something we'd normally carry," she said when her pulse had slowed to the still-too-fast rate it seemed to maintain around him, "but Mrs. Walker has been a customer for years, and it's not that much trouble."

"Specialized."

"It's what we do."

"Rare."

She bristled slightly. "If you're going to suggest I stop such things, forget it."

He lifted a brow at her. "Wouldn't. You know your business."

She took a breath. "Thank you. The efficiency expert dad consulted a couple of years ago, after he got sick, was always telling him things like that."

"Destroy what made you."

"Exactly," she said, warmed by his grasp of what she'd tried to tell the man from Portland who had bustled about the crowded aisles and piled shelves with a sort of distaste that reminded her of a pansified prig faced with a mud puddle.

"I'm feeling a bit harried," she said. "Sorry I snarled."

He looked surprised. He knew she was under pressure, so it had to be the apology that had startled him.

"Didn't snarl. Couldn't."

Her breath caught; he'd said it like someone who had known her for years.

And there she was, back in the deep water she'd been trying so hard not to plunge into. Had he remembered her? Had he thought of her, over the years, when he'd been wherever he'd been, doing whatever he'd done? Or had he lumped her in with all the ugly memories of that time and this place, things to be forgotten, erased, washed away as the flooding river had washed away so much that long-ago night?

With an effort, she made herself focus on the here and now.

"I heard something interesting yesterday," she said. He waited silently. "Ran into Joe Winston, who works at the bank in River Mill. He was quite rushed, he said, because it seems the bank is being audited."

"Happens." His expression betrayed nothing, but she knew.

"He said the only thing they've turned up so far is a data-entry clerk who apparently made some errors posting payments."

He still said nothing.

"It probably would have ended there, but they found out that same clerk had made some large cash deposits in his own account at about the same time as the errors were made."

"Stupid."

"Yes." She waited, but he was apparently determined not to be lured into admitting anything. So she went on. "The clerk at the post office told me there's been a reporter from the *Ledger,* the big county newspaper, nosing around. Asking about Alden's finances, his dealings, even his wife's suicide and…his son's death."

That at least got more words out of him. "Real investigative journalism?"

She leaned against the front counter, keeping her gaze on him steadily. "Not much call for that these days, is there?" she said, almost conversationally. "Why do you suppose they care about our little election, when there's much bigger news on the county level?"

He gave her a one-shouldered shrug that told her nothing, but the fact that he didn't meet her eyes told her much more.

"But the most interesting thing I heard this week, while you were…wherever you were, is that Mr. Alden had a very strange reaction to a large personal loan he made suddenly being paid back in full."

"Did he." The low, soft-voiced words were not a question.

"He was furious. One of his clients was in his office when the phone call came, and heard it all. He was, apparently, screaming that whoever he'd loaned the money to couldn't get out of their deal so easily. That he owned him."

Something came into his eyes then, something dark and deep and deadly. It was there only an instant, but it made a chill sweep through her, and the old joke about being someone's worst nightmare suddenly wasn't funny anymore.

He owned him….

She shuddered as she thought of the other contexts those words could be used in, contexts that could have caused that look in his eyes. And she understood.

"Do not vote for me because you loved my father, or because you feel tradition demands having a Hill in the mayor's office. Although I appreciate the sentiments, those are not good reasons to entrust me with the future of Cedar. Trust me, vote for me because I share your vision of what we want this town we love to be. Because I, like you, want us to proceed into the future without losing the parts of the past that make us what we are."

It was good, St. John thought. She was reaching the crowd. And there was a crowd. Not as big as her opponent's, perhaps, but they were more attentive. He was guessing they were the ones who were more aware, more active.

"I'm not a politician, you all know that," Jenna was saying, "because I won't make promises I can't keep, just to get your vote. I won't make backroom deals that result in policies that help the loudest group. I won't try to buy this office—it has to be earned."

That got, as he'd expected, a bit of applause and a lot of buzz started. And that was encouraging, that they so quickly realized what she meant.

It also had an effect he'd expected; a man yelled out, "Why should we trust you, when you can't even run your family business?"

St. John spotted the man, recognized him as an Alden plant he'd seen in the opposition's campaign headquarters. A man from River Mill, not Cedar. His gaze shot to Jessa, willing her to keep her cool.

She laughed. "Why, if you lived here in Cedar you would have seen that I posted our profit and loss statements right in the store window, so everyone could see that we're actually doing even a little better than last year."

Yes!

The triumphant word shot through him as she handled it perfectly, beautifully. In one sentence she countered his false accusation, and pointed out to the crowd that he wasn't one of them. Her gaze flicked to him, and he read the acknowledgment in her eyes; he'd anticipated this, and that was why she'd posted those figures for all to see.

"We could do better, of course, if we charged more, carried no specialty items, but we think our customers are special, and deserve the same kind of service we've provided for decades. The same kind of service you'll get from the mayor's office."

That neatly, she brought it back to the matter at hand, and this time the applause outweighed the buzz.

"Hey, he works for Bracken's!" someone yelled out.

And suddenly the tenor of the meeting changed. They were on her side now, local girl versus outsider, and they were looking at the intruder in their midst with suspicion. The man looked uncomfortable, and began to back out of the crowd amid the murmurs. He wasn't a pro, St. John thought, or he would have stuck it out, been better prepared.

Alden, he thought, wasn't going to like this. Which was exactly what he wanted. Because he knew too well what Albert Alden did when confronted with things he didn't like.

Chapter 15

"**I**'ve never seen anything like it," Marion Wagman was saying. "To scream at the poor woman like that, out on a public street."

Mrs. Walker, shifting the bags full of groceries she held, shook her head. "It's hardly Janelle's fault that the bank is being audited."

"She was very upset, I'll tell you. Said that he didn't even bank there until a couple of years ago, but acts like he owns it. And the employees."

Jessa kept her head down, studying the boxes of cake mix as if they held the answers to all the mysteries of the world. When the women left the store, she wheeled her cart to the checkout, her mind racing.

When she got home, she found her mother bustling in the kitchen, a pleasant surprise, and her uncle sitting in the breakfast nook, a cup of coffee before him.

"Hello, honey." She kissed Jessa on the cheek as she took the bag of requested items. "Thank you."

"Sure, Mom."

"Next time I'll do it, I promise."

Jessa looked into her mother's eyes, so like her brother-in-law's, minus the slightly fey quality. They did seem a bit brighter, more alive today, and if Uncle Larry had accomplished that, she was thankful.

"They'll be happy to see you at the market," she said, knowing it was true.

"Sit down, visit with your uncle. I'll get you some coffee."

Jessa glanced at the man at the table, saw the very slight nod he gave her, and did as her mother had suggested. The coffeemaker was at the other end of the kitchen, and gave them a few moments to speak unheard.

"Thank you."

Larry smiled. "Time, not man, is the true healer."

"But you're helping."

"Perhaps." Then, as his sister-in-law approached with two steaming mugs, he shifted subjects. "Heard an interesting rumor in town this morning."

"Is this about Alden's public meltdown? I heard," Jessa said, secretly delighted that her mother had joined them; too often she simply retreated, a shadow of her once vibrant self.

Larry lifted a brow at her. "Now, I hadn't heard that one. What happened?"

She relayed what she'd overheard, adding as she finished, "It's really not like him. He's too conscious of his public image."

"And more charming than any honest man needs to be," Naomi put in.

Jessa held her breath; it had been so long since her mother had offered an opinion on even the weather, let alone anything requiring more thought, that she was afraid to speak lest she destroy the moment.

"Quite true," Larry said smoothly. "A man with no rough edges is either a fake or has worked on the outside until it's slippery, neglecting the inside."

Jessa couldn't stop her grin at that. "Uncle Larry, you are one of a kind."

"Blessedly so," he said, grinning back at her. "Only room for one Loony Larry in this little town."

The careless ease with which he accepted the disrespectful nickname the less charitable citizens had given him long ago was just another of the reasons she adored this man. Their inability to see the wisdom hidden in some of his more outlandish statements was their loss, she thought.

The idea flashed through her mind that following Uncle Larry's flights of fancy had been good preparation for following St. John's choppy shorthand.

"So what was it you heard?" she asked him. "Was it the reporter thing?"

"Heard that, too," Larry said, "but that's not what I meant."

"What reporter?" her mother asked.

"From the *Ledger*," Jessa said. "Nosing into Alden's life."

"Interesting," Larry said. "I wonder what brought it on, why the sudden interest on the county level?"

Jessa had an idea, just as she had on the bank's audit, and they both had St. John's name on them. But she didn't say anything. She had no proof, after all.

"Well, whatever the reason it's a good thing, after the shabby way the *Cedar Report* has treated you," her mother said, surprising her. She hadn't thought her mother was aware of that much of what had been going on. "I'm so disappointed in them. We've always supported them, and then they endorse that…charlatan."

"They didn't have much choice," Jessa said. "Turns out Alden owns a sizeable piece of them."

"Why…that's outrageous!" her mother exclaimed. "They shouldn't have endorsed anyone, then."

"Just how," Larry asked, looking at her thoughtfully

over his mug of coffee, "did you pick up that little bit of information?"

"I didn't, really," she said.

"Ah. Our mysterious friend and benefactor."

She'd almost forgotten Larry had been there the first day St. John had arrived. And although to her knowledge that was all he'd seen of the man, her uncle had a remarkable knack for sizing people up quickly.

"Yes," she admitted.

"And the rest?"

"Maybe. I don't know for sure."

"I suspect he's capable of moving mountains of any ilk," Larry mused in his not-quite-in-the-present way.

"Wouldn't surprise me," Jessa said, her mouth quirking.

"Who is this?" her mother asked.

"A man who's helping," she said. "It's a long story, Mom," she added at her mother's curious look. "I hope to be able to tell it all to you soon."

Her mother's gaze switched to her brother. "Larry?"

"I'm watching," he said.

Touched by her mother's concern, more that she had bestirred herself to feel it, Jessa swallowed past the tightness in her throat. She noted her mother's nod and the easing of her concern, and envied her uncle that knack, as well.

And wondered exactly what he'd meant, if he was watching her, the situation or St. John. Or all three.

"We still haven't gotten to what you heard, Uncle Lare," she said.

"Ah. Rumor has it someone's made an offer on Riverside Paper."

Jessa's brow furrowed. "An offer? I didn't know it was for sale."

"It wasn't, but in these times solid money talks. And if what I heard is true, this is very solid money."

"That must be worrying for all the people who work there," her mother said. Jessa felt an odd combination of emotions at the words. Gratitude that her mother was participating so much this morning, and a dull ache because those would have been her father's first words, as well.

"Actually, not so much," Larry said.

"But if some outsider is taking over," Jessa began.

"Yes. But that outsider is Redstone."

Jessa blinked. "What? What on earth would they want with a paper company way out here?"

"Redstone?" her mother said. "You mean Joshua Redstone? Jess admired him greatly. But don't they do airplanes, resorts, that sort of thing?"

"And dabble in highly advanced prosthetics, medical equipment, high-tech gadgets, whatever their R & D department comes up with," Larry said. "I'd give a lot to meet their inventor. Not a lot of genuine inventors around anymore. Everything's done by committee."

"You seem to know a lot about them," Jessa said.

Larry shrugged. "They're fascinating. A powerhouse, privately owned company that size that is run the way it is, whose people sing its praises with no prompting, and that seems to spread benefits in ripples wherever it goes...."

"I've heard that," Jessa agreed. "But I still don't understand why they'd want to come here."

"That, I don't know," Larry agreed. "They've not dabbled in that particular line, that I'm aware of. Which makes this all the more interesting."

Especially given Alden's huge investment in Riverside Paper, she thought. And it occurred to her, somewhat belatedly, to wonder if all this wasn't connected.

At the idea, a string of images popped into her head. St. John, muttering about phone calls and vanishing. St. John, turning up the information on those investments.

St. John, saying with cold, deadly certainty, "I will destroy him."

A new emotion filled her as the implications roiled around in her mind; utter awe. Was it truly possible? Could one man have done all this so quickly? Even a man as driven and intense as St. John?

He could if he had the weight of Redstone behind him, she thought.

It was a leap, she knew, but not necessarily a blind one.

I will destroy him.

She shivered inwardly. He'd meant every word. She'd understood, accepted, even welcomed the thought; after all, she'd gone into this to stop Alden, not because she wanted the office.

But there was one last image she couldn't quite put out of her mind, and it might just be the one that would trump all else. It was of a young boy, hesitantly, longingly looking at a big golden dog.

A young boy who was trapped just as St. John had once been, in Alden's twisted world.

"You think you can get away with this?"

Jessa instinctively stepped back, regretted the cowardly action, and covered it by wiping at her face. "You're spraying," she said with a distaste she didn't have to feign.

She'd known it would infuriate the man, but they were standing in front of the copy store, with several curious early-morning onlookers, and she felt relatively safe. Especially since one of them was Uncle Larry, who, curiously, was standing back silently. But then she saw Alden's right hand curl into a fist, and suddenly wondered if she'd pushed him too hard.

"You're behind all this," he hissed. "This is all your fault."

"I don't do conspiracy theories before noon," Jessa said, earning a laugh from the onlookers, who were growing in number. Which only made Alden redden even more; he was not a man who took kindly to being laughed at. She had the feeling he was barely managing not to strike out at her, or even at those who had chuckled.

"I don't know how you've managed to do it, but I'll find out." He nearly spat it out again.

"Mr. Alden," she said, in the tone of a parent explaining to a child his flaw in logic, "you simply cannot have it both ways. I'm either too stupid to run the family business, or I'm brilliant enough to have put together whatever conspiracy it is you're accusing me of."

She glanced at the small crowd, saw her uncle grinning at her proudly. She heard the murmur, knew her point had registered with those who mattered, those who would then tell their friends, their families. She knew Cedar, knew how it worked. This was the town where when Adam Alden had allegedly—she knew he hadn't, because he'd been with her—sprayed graffiti on the Welcome to Cedar sign, everyone had known about it before the paint even dried.

Which brought her to the true irony of this encounter; Albert Alden could very well be, in a way, right about her being behind his troubles.

As the man swore at her and then departed, with a sharp bark of the tires on his expensive Swedish sedan, she heard the murmurings of the people who'd been drawn by the unusual—for Cedar anyway—disturbance. She saw among them Missy Wagman who, besides being the first to jump on any new bandwagon of negativity, was also the main server on the exceedingly efficient Cedar information network. Word of this encounter would be all over before Jessa even got to the store with the box of file folders she'd stopped to pick up.

She looked at the group, who were either shaking their heads in shock or nodding in agreement. Except for Larry, who was looking at her with such approval in his eyes that she felt a flood of encouragement.

"Hope he doesn't take that mad out on Tyler." *Like he used to take them out on Adam,* she added to herself.

She saw the comment register, saw the frowns, the furrowed brows, knew that some of them, at least, were wondering.

"Two accident-prone sons?"

Uncle Larry had said it, in that vague, thoughtful way of his, as if it were simply a curiosity. But there was nothing vague in his expression, and Jessa knew he'd done it with full intent.

"And one of them dead," someone said, eliciting another round of murmurs. Some of the group were too young to remember, but many had also gone to school with her and with Adam, and would remember his endless parade of bruises and injuries.

"Not to mention a wife who committed suicide," Missy muttered, true to form and jumping on the newly formed, questioning bandwagon.

Larry moved then, taking Jessa's arm. "Come along, honey," he said, adding when they were out of earshot, "our work here is done."

She looked at his face, and nearly laughed at his satisfied grin.

"I'm proud of you, girl. You handled that perfectly, turned an attack into an advantage, and gave people a glimpse of the real man. A glimpse they'll remember." He shifted his arm to drape it over her shoulders and give them a squeeze. "More important, your father would be proud. Because you also handled it with class."

The words meant more to her than she could manage to tell him past the knot in her throat. She fought tears, slipped her arm around his waist, and hugged him as they stopped on the corner and waited for one of Cedar's three traffic signals to change so they could cross the street.

"I love you, Uncle Larry."

"I know. An accomplishment, since I don't make it easy."

"It's easy for me," she said. "And anybody who thinks for themselves."

"That would be you," Larry said, pleasing her all over again.

But the feeling faded, replaced by concern. "I meant what I said, though. I hope he doesn't take this out on poor Tyler."

"I've been keeping an eye on the lad," Larry said as they got the green light. "He visits, now and then."

Her eyes widened; she hadn't known. "You never said."

They headed down the last block to the store. "He asked me not to. Couldn't betray that."

"Of course not." Her uncle had always been a safe repository for any childhood secret. And she guessed Tyler had a few. Just as Adam had. "I'm glad he comes to you."

"He likes the gnomes. And they like him."

Jessa laughed as they reached the back entrance to the store and paused while she dug the keys out of her pocket. "Don't ever change, Uncle Larry."

"That's not," he said solemnly, "what most of the world would say."

"Their loss," she said, hugging him again.

"I'll go check on your mother," he said. "I think I may be able to get her to go with me over to Stanton's this morning."

"That would be wonderful. She—"

Jessa stopped abruptly. She'd stuck the key in the back door lock automatically, focused more on her uncle than the task. But that hadn't prevented her from realizing something was wrong.

The door was already unlocked.

She frowned, puzzled. "I know I locked up yesterday."

"Of course you did," Larry said, moving between her and the unsecured door. "You always do."

It was his movement rather than his words that drew her full, sharpened attention. The meaning of it hit her abruptly. Along with two possibilities. And she didn't like either one of them.

Either this damned campaign had escalated to true nastiness, or a serious sort of crime had come to her beloved Cedar.

"You think someone broke in?" she said, her voice dropping to a whisper.

"I think we'll be careful until we know." He reached for the door handle.

"The sheriff," she began, reaching for the cell phone in her purse.

"Is a half hour away, as usual," Larry said as he pressed the release lever.

She knew the old joke was true out here; when seconds counted, the police were only minutes away. It was why people here were generally self-reliant. They had to be.

"Alden?" she asked.

"Perhaps." He glanced at the cell phone. "That thing have a camera on it?"

"Of course."

"Might be good to have a record."

"And a weapon," she said grimly.

She darted over to one of the outside racks and grabbed up two of the big garden stakes that were sharpened for pushing into the ground; in a pinch they could be lethal. And she was getting mad now. Whichever possibility was true, she wasn't going to let it go unchallenged.

Larry read her expression, gave her a quick nod of approval that was like a salute. He took one of the stakes.

"Let's find out what's going on here," she whispered.

Chapter 16

There was a light on in the office. She could see it from back here, in the section of the store that held the candles and lamp oil they carried for when the power went out. Cedar was on the outer edge of the grid, and often the last to be restored, so that self-reliance wasn't just useful, it was necessary.

She knew she hadn't left that light on, just as she knew she hadn't failed to lock the back door.

They moved quietly through aisles they both knew well, avoiding the decorative wind chimes and sticking to the concrete floor rather than the wood section of the older side. Larry paused just outside the open office door. Jessa held her breath. She could hear faint tapping noises from inside. Then they stopped.

"Breathe."

The word came from inside and was as much command as comment, but for an instant Jessa couldn't. But she felt Larry relax, and finally managed to draw in that needed air.

St. John.

"I should have known," she muttered.

"Car's parked." The tapping resumed.

"We came from the other direction, not past the parking lot," Larry said mildly, stepping into the office, Jessa on his heels. And once she was inside, she almost forgot to breathe all over again.

"What," she said, staring, "are you doing?"

"Finishing."

He was staring at a computer monitor, his fingers flying over a keyboard. Neither of which belonged here, or had been here when she'd closed last night.

But of even more concern was the fact that it seemed nearly all of the stores files were piled all over the office. And all thought of asking him how he'd gotten in here vanished.

He made a half dozen more keystrokes, entered a save command, then stood up and gestured at the chair he'd vacated.

"Sit."

"I am not Maui," she snapped.

He blinked, as if startled. "Please," he added, as if that was all that was bothering her. When she didn't move, he reached out and took her arm, as if to guide her, as if she didn't understand what he wanted her to do. The contact seared through her, making her resent this, and him, all the more. Why couldn't she keep her head straight around this guy?

Because you never could, she reminded herself. She made an effort to pull herself together.

"What. Are. You. Doing?"

He looked puzzled by her careful enunciation. He glanced at Larry as if her uncle held the answer to her odd behavior. But Larry was simply watching, an oddly amused expression on his face. Clearly he wasn't suspecting St. John of anything nefarious, even if he did have the guts of Hill's spread all over the room.

"Inputting," he said, indicating the piles with a hand gesture that silently added the words, "Of course." As if she should have realized.

"What into what? And if you can indeed speak in full sentences," Jessa added, "this would be a very good time to demonstrate."

"Your data. Software's ready."

For all its terseness, that was, for him, two complete sentences. It probably would normally have been "Data. Software." Two whole extra words.

"Software," she repeated. She looked at the equipment now on her desk. There was no brand name on it, but it was obviously new. "How about the hardware?"

"This, for now. More, if you like it."

"I—we—can't afford this."

"Later. Look," he said, again gesturing at the chair, and this time adding more quickly, "please."

"I'll run along and check on your mother, girl. You two children play nice."

Her uncle's teasing words sent a flash of memory shooting through her, of one of those long-ago summer days by the river, when she had realized Adam didn't play. At anything. He didn't even fantasize about the future. It was only later that she'd understood that the sweetness of childhood play was something he'd never been allowed to learn, and you couldn't fantasize about a future you didn't think you were ever going to see.

Slowly, she sat in the chair.

Within minutes she realized several things. First, the computer she was sitting at was fast, powerful and high-end. Second, the software it was running was a dream come true; it did every last thing she'd wanted and a few more she hadn't even thought of. Third, and perhaps most startling, it appeared that every bit of the store's information had already been entered.

This time when she spoke, she was looking at him with more than a little awe. "What have you done? Have you been working on this all night?"

"Most," he said.

He didn't look or act particularly tired, certainly not like she would be if she had done a marathon like this. The only sign at all was his stubbled jaw, a bit more than the day he'd first arrived here. The look had never appealed to her that much.

Until now.

She stared at him. "I don't know what to say. How to... thank you."

He shrugged. "Thank Barton."

"I will, whoever and wherever he is. But all the work you did—"

The shrug again. "Grunt work."

"It would have taken me forever," she said. "Because I would have been..."

This time, when she almost wished he would interrupt her, he didn't. But after a moment of her silence he said softly, "Hurting."

Her eyes widened. And for the third time this morning she nearly forgot to breathe.

"You knew," she said, her voice tiny. "You knew how much it would hurt, because of all the disagreements my father and I had over this."

And for the third time he shrugged. "Done."

"Why?" she asked, still watching him intently.

"Needed it."

"So you just decided to break in here in the middle of the night like some good little elf and take care of it all?"

"Goblin."

"What?"

"More goblin than elf."

She blinked. Had he just made a joke? Before she could react, a scratching came at the back door. Uncle Larry must have let Maui out, and he'd come over to check on her. That the dog felt able to leave her mother again this morning was a good sign, she told herself.

She started to get up, but St. John stopped her, indicating

with a gesture that he'd get the door for Maui. With another gesture at the computer monitor, he conveyed perfectly well, if silently, that he wanted her to continue to explore the new setup.

Which, to be honest, was exactly what she wanted to do. She couldn't quite believe it was all here, everything she'd wanted, as if it had truly been custom tailored for her and for Hill's. Which, apparently, it had.

She heard Maui's happy bark of greeting; the big golden had no reservations about St. John. That comforted her, as did the whimsical notion that somehow the dog knew his grandfather had once adored this man, as well.

To her amazement, she heard St. John greet the dog in turn, using nearly complete sentences.

"Morning, Maui. Come to check on her? Good. She needs you, too, now."

She paused in her explorations to greet the sweet-hearted animal, then went back to the computer. She was aware—very aware—of St. John standing in the office doorway, but he seemed content enough to simply watch as she marveled over each new facet she discovered. When she found she could not only cross-reference the customer list with inventory, but the inventory with any number of possible suppliers she wanted, she couldn't help exclaiming about it.

"Bot," St. John said.

She glanced at him. "What?"

"A bot. Checks supplier Web sites periodically. Specials, deals."

Her gaze whipped back to the screen. "It will do that?"

"Slowly," he said, with a grimace. "Working on that."

She looked back at him. "Going to personally run high-speed fiber optics all the way out here?" Somehow it didn't seem at all unbelievable.

"Settle for DSL."

"I'd be delighted with DSL. I—"

"Jessa!"

Her mother's voice startled her out of whatever she'd been going to say. Naomi Hill hadn't set foot in the store of her own volition in weeks, and Jessa didn't know whether the fact that she had now was good or bad. Judging by the urgent tone of her voice, she was leaning toward the latter.

"Jessa! Are you all right?"

Her mother appeared in the office doorway. She gave St. John a curious look, but her focus was on her daughter. Jessa crossed the office quickly.

"I'm fine, Mom. What's wrong?"

"Larry told me that you had a run-in with Al Alden this morning."

Jessa didn't look at St. John, but then she didn't have to; she sensed his sudden tension, felt his newly sharpened gaze on her as if it were a physical connection between them.

"It was nothing, really, Mom."

"That's not what Larry said. He said the man accused you of some kind of conspiracy against him."

She managed to get out a credible laugh. "And you can imagine how crazy that made him sound. It was nothing, Mom. In fact, it just made him look bad in front of Mrs. Walker and a few others."

Seemingly reassured now that her daughter was intact and relatively unscathed, Naomi let out a compressed breath that actually sounded angry.

"That man," she said, with a fierceness that warmed Jessa, both for the love it implied, and the simple fact of it's reappearance after so long. "I never quite trusted him, no matter how well he charmed everyone else in this town."

Jessa chose her next words with care, as much for the man listening so intently as for her mother. "I know. I remember you saying so when I was a kid."

St. John went even more still, seeming to barely breathe now.

Naomi was patting her arm now. "But Larry said you were brilliant. That you made a fool of him, pointing out that he couldn't spread lies about you being not smart enough to be mayor and then turn around and say you were clever enough to engineer whatever all his problems are."

"He opened the door for that one himself," Jessa said with a smile and a hug for the woman who had apparently rediscovered at least some bit of life outside her own horrible grief.

"Yes. Well."

Her mother suddenly seemed to recall they were not alone. She turned to look at the man in the doorway, who hadn't spoken a word. Not that that fooled Jessa; she knew he'd taken in every bit of what had been said.

"You must be our mysterious benefactor," her mother was saying to St. John. "I don't believe I've heard your name, just that you appeared one day."

There was no real accusation in her tone, but she still had a bit of the demeanor of a mother protecting her child. Something St. John had never known, Jessa realized. And yet he responded to it just the same.

To her amazement, he introduced himself with an old-world kind of grace and civility—and full, elegant sentences—she wouldn't have thought the brusque, taciturn man he'd become capable of.

"Dameron St. John, Mrs. Hill." He took her hand gently, with the slightest of bows over it. "It's a true honor. And my deepest condolences, heartfelt."

Jessa gaped at him, while her mother gave him a startled smile. Then, as the older woman looked up at the dark, younger man, something odd came into her eyes, something puzzled.

"You remind me of someone," she murmured.

Jessa saw him go very still. He straightened and backed up a step. But he said nothing more, as if those three complete sentences had drained him of any words at all. And only then did she notice Uncle Larry was standing in the doorway, watching this odd little tableau with that fey sort of interest that made her wonder anew just what he was seeing.

"You can see the girl's fine, now, Naomi. Let's be going. It will be good for you—and for Jessa—if you're seen out and about. And your friends miss you."

Her mother didn't look happy about whatever he'd persuaded her to do. "I don't know—"

"One small step, Mom," Jessa said. "Just a start. Then come home. Stay inside for a week, if you want."

She gave in at last, and let Larry lead the way out the door. Maui watched them, then looked at Jessa. "Go," she said. "It will distract her to watch out for you."

The dog trotted after them as if he'd understood every word. And Jessa wasn't at all sure he hadn't.

"Who's watching who?"

She looked at him, then saw, as usual, nothing she could read in his face. But his eyes held a wary, edgy look.

"I'm not sure it matters," she said.

They spent the rest of the morning going over the computer program in detail, interrupted occasionally by a customer.

"Need help," he said as, unasked, he helped her load several bags of garden soil into the back of a pickup.

"I have Greg Walker around in the afternoons, after school. He's a good worker."

"More."

"I like working." Although she had to admit the twelve-hour days and frequent nights spent on paperwork were beginning to wear on her. Although that, she thought, might just change, thanks to the amazing computer system he'd installed, and that she still didn't quite know how to thank him for.

"Distraction."

"Yes. Problem?"

He stopped for a moment, whether at her tone or her mimicking of his speech pattern, she wasn't sure. But before either of them could speak, another customer called out from inside the store.

"I'll finish," he said.

She hesitated, then nodded; there were only two bags left anyway. "You're all set, Mr. Cardenas," she told the pickup's owner, an elderly gentleman with gardening gloves sticking out of his back pocket. "Will Matt be home to help you unload?"

"I'll wait until he is," the man said with a grin. "No point in breaking my back when my grandson's trying to beef up for the football team."

Jessa laughed. "Give him my best, and good luck to him," she said, then headed inside.

She found Catherine Parker, a teacher from North Side Elementary, at the counter with a stack of cans of the expensive cat food Jessa always stocked for her. She was the only one who bought the stuff, but she bought enough of it every week—Jessa didn't want to know how many cats the woman actually had—so that they actually broke even on it.

"They're making cat treats now," Jessa said as she wrote up the sale, thinking how much easier it would be to simply enter it in that amazing new software. The software with the bot that had found out that bit of information about the treats in its first perusal of the company's Web site.

"Really? The furry kids would love that. Could you order some?"

"Of course," she said, smiling inwardly, thinking that the fancy system had already begun to pay for itself. She would order the treats this afternoon, when she reordered the food, and then—

"—busy morning, what with Tyler Alden and all."

Jessa suddenly tuned back in to Catherine's chatter. "What?"

"You didn't hear? Poor kid, showed up at school today with a broken arm. Fell out of that old maple tree in their yard. Must have landed on his face, too, school nurse says he's going to have a black eye."

Reckless kid, that Adam Alden. Always falling and hurting himself.

Another black eye? That boy's always fighting.

He's bruised up again? Wonder what he ran into this time?

The words from long ago beat at her, and as she had then, she wanted to scream at those long-ago voices, "Can't you see? He's *not* clumsy, he's not fighting, at least not like you mean."

"Jessa? Are you all right?"

"Fine," she said mechanically. "You just reminded me of something I need to do."

The woman left with a promise to stop by and pick up the cat treats as soon as they came in. Jessa just stood there for a moment, staring at nothing.

"Jess?"

She didn't even jump at his quiet voice behind her. Didn't react to his use of the nickname that he, who noticed everything, didn't seem to realize betrayed him. She was too enveloped by an old, aching pain. But this time, she wasn't a child who could be convinced to remain quiet, this time she wasn't a child who knew what she should do but didn't know how to do it without causing even more pain to someone she cared about so much.

She turned to look at him. "Tyler Alden arrived at school today with a broken arm and a black eye. He said he fell. Out of that old maple tree."

She knew how it would hit him, because she remembered too well that he'd used that story once himself, one among many. And it did hit him; he didn't just go quiet and still, he went rigid.

"I made his father angry this morning, and he took it out on the most defenseless person under his control. You know how it works."

He swore under his breath.

"He took it out on Tyler," she said, and then, before she'd

even realized she'd decided it was time, she added the words that would change everything.

"Just like he used to take it out on you."

Chapter 17

She knew.

St. John couldn't deny the shiver that went through him. That it was tinged not just with relief, but a strange sort of pleasure rattled him. He'd been so certain no one would ever recognize him, yet had, he admitted now, secretly wished one person would.

This one.

He considered, for all of a split second, denying it. But he doubted it would work. She was looking at him steadily, holding his gaze in an unflinching manner even those at Redstone rarely did.

Oh, she knew, all right. And nothing he said would convince her she was wrong, he could see that in those beautiful, changeable eyes.

Besides, he didn't *want* to deny it. Not to her. To everyone else, but not to her.

Finally he, who was never the first to blink, lowered his gaze.

"How long?" he asked, startled at the sound of his own voice, at the strain he heard in the quiet question.

"Since that day in the cemetery."

His head came up sharply, his gaze shooting back to her face. That long?

"Why?"

She followed his jump, as she seemed able to do better than some who'd had a lot more practice.

"Why didn't I say something before?" At his slight nod, she answered, "No one knew better than I that you had good reason to not want to be recognized here. Especially by one man."

"Didn't."

"I know he didn't recognize you. Looking at his own son, face-to-face, he didn't. But then, he hasn't spent the last twenty years wishing you'd somehow come back."

And suddenly his throat was so tight he could barely breathe. And again he had to look away.

"Why?" he managed.

"Because until my father got sick, nothing else in my entire life had gone so wrong." She took a breath, as if to steady herself to go on. "Or been so precious and then lost."

He felt another shiver go through him, knew this one was visible, but couldn't bring himself to care if she saw it. Not Jess. She had always known his darkest secrets, and they had ever and always been safe with her. He'd never trusted anyone as he trusted her. He'd trust Josh with just about anything, his life even, but this woman, who even as a child had had a wisdom far beyond her years, had been the only one he'd trusted with the dark shadows of his soul.

"Not fair."

"That my good, loving father is gone while your vicious, evil one lives on? Oh, yes, it's beyond unfair."

There was no answer to that sad truth. Then, finally, he got to the crux of it, the one thing he'd been afraid to ask. And because he realized, with a little shock, that he was afraid, he made himself ask.

"How?"

"How could I not? I only felt a fool because it took me so long to realize there could only be one pair of eyes like that in this world. And they belonged to the one person who has haunted two-thirds of my life. Adam Alden."

He winced at the sound of the name he hadn't heard applied directly to him in that two-thirds of her lifetime. She caught it, and spoke quickly.

"I'm sorry. I don't blame you for wanting to wash your hands of everything that tainted you from this place."

"Not everything," he said, so low he wasn't even sure she'd heard it.

There was a pause before she spoke. And for a moment he was afraid of what she might say, that whatever words came would somehow make it worse, make him realize he'd not accomplished the only real thing he'd wanted to before he'd gone. She had to know, he thought. She had to know that the only thing he regretted leaving behind when he'd escaped this place was her.

She didn't say it. Instead, she said simply, "I'll try not to slip up on the name again. You must hate it."

"His arrogance." He sucked in a breath. "Thinks he's God."

Again she made the jump with him. "So he named his son after God's firstborn, as it were?" Her mouth twisted, her expression sour. "I hadn't thought of it like that."

He couldn't speak.

"Definitely lose the name, then," she said, briskly, as if to shake off the feeling. "But I admit, I can't quite get used to calling you just St. John. Dameron?"

He'd known he'd regret that, but her mother had deserved a full introduction, to ease her fears. It had been the least he could do for the woman who had always been kind to him, when others assumed he was everything his father had to nobly endure.

And Jess deserved an explanation. She was the only person on this planet outside of Redstone who did.

"Dameron. Dam." He gave her a sideways look. "Fit."

Her mouth quirked at that. "Let's hope when it comes to your father, it's a verb."

He blinked. And then, slowly, unable to help himself, he smiled. Her eyes widened. And then she smiled back, and in that moment, the two kids they'd once been greeted each other once more.

When she turned, walked to the front of the store and flipped the Open sign to the Closed side, he knew he was in for it. He realized when she was back that he could have escaped while she'd been doing it, but it hadn't occurred to him. More proof of how rattled he was.

"How did you come up with that name?" was her first question when she was back.

He knew he had to answer. This was Jessa. She deserved it. And more.

"Walked to River Mill. Hitched to Grant's Pass. Bus. Driver was St. John. California. First street sign I saw."

"Was…Dameron Street?"

He nodded.

"Why California?"

"Where the first bus was going."

"What did you do? You were only fourteen."

He shrugged. "Ways."

"I'm sure there are, but—" Her words broke off sharply. He flicked a glance at her face, read the horror that was dawning.

And realized, as he'd feared that day in the cemetery, she knew everything. He'd hoped, somehow, that she hadn't guessed the details of his final degradation, that she'd been too young, too innocent, too pure to even conceive of it. And perhaps she had been, then. But she was too smart not to have realized, eventually. He should have known.

"No," he said, fighting the churning in his gut. "Not that. Never again. Swore I'd die first."

She moved then. Quickly. So quickly he didn't have time to move, to dodge. And then her arms were around him, her warmth enveloping him. He stiffened, resisting, but she held on, and she was stronger than he'd realized. Strong enough that if he forced it, he could hurt her.

And with a jolt that nearly took his breath away he realized he didn't want to. Realized that instead of fighting her, his own arms had encircled her as if of their own volition. But he knew that wasn't true, knew that on some level he'd wanted this from the moment he'd walked into this place and seen her again. Little Jessa Hill, all grown up, a change that, sillily, had shocked him.

"It's a pleasure to meet you, Dameron St. John," she whispered.

"Jess," he murmured, unable to say anything more.

He was half-sitting on the edge of the desk, and she was locked in his arms, leaning against him. He felt an odd flood of sensation, as if somehow she had the power to give him back some of the innocence and hope she'd always had in abundance and he'd never known. At the same time, his body was very aware it was a soft, warm, sweet woman he held. It had responded swiftly, fiercely, before he could rein in the response. He who controlled so much, most of all himself, couldn't seem to control anything about his responses to her. His emotions, and now his body, were running amok. And if she so much as moved she was going to realize that.

"What happened then?" The question came quietly, muffled slightly because she was pressed against his chest. He wondered if she could hear his heart slamming in his chest, rocketing out of control.

Out of control.

God, no one at Redstone would believe it, they wouldn't

recognize the legendary St. John, reduced to this at the mere touch of a little blond pixie who had haunted his years just as she'd said he'd haunted hers.

He wanted to answer as St. John would, to tell her, in as few words as possible, that it was none of her concern, that he didn't talk about it, wouldn't talk about it, and then move on to business.

He couldn't. This was Jessa, and he couldn't.

With one of the greatest efforts of his life, he fought against twenty years of ingrained conditioning, twenty years of isolating himself, of keeping the world at bay. He'd never thought about how he would tell his story, because he'd never expected to tell it.

"Start," he muttered.

"Beginning," she suggested, again as if his single word responses were catching. "That night," she added then, "you planned it all?"

"Yes. Nature had other plans. Really fell."

She jerked back sharply, stared up into his face. "Into the river?"

He nodded. "Slipped on the rock."

He didn't have to explain which one. He knew she'd know he meant the huge boulder where they often sat, in a hollowed-out section that formed a comfortable spot.

Her gaze shifted to the scar along his jaw. He nodded. "That edge."

The mostly smooth boulder had also had a jagged edge where a section had broken off, and it had been that that sliced open his face when he'd slid over it in his tumble into the swirling water.

"That explains why they found skin and blood there," she said.

"Yes. Rain had stopped by then."

"You knew?"

"Later. Looked up newspapers."

She settled back against him, and he relaxed, only then

realizing he'd been afraid she would pull away. The knowledge rattled him even further, and he wondered if he was going to survive this. But she had the right to hear it. She was the only one who did.

"The rest?" she said after a minute of silence.

He nearly shuddered under the effort, and when the words finally came, they were like the staccato bursts of a machine gun.

"Four years surviving. Bad company. Learned a lot, good and bad. No jail, barely. Moved around." He took a breath, amazed at how much this was taking out of him. "Met a man. He...helped."

What a paucity of acknowledgment for what Josh had done for him, he thought. It bordered on insult, and he couldn't let it go at that.

"He...saved my life."

He felt her go still, seeming to even stop breathing. "Figuratively?" she asked.

"And literally. Eighteenth birthday. The real one. Was going to...finish what started that night."

He thought about it rarely, and never spoke of it at all, but now that he had, it rose up and engulfed him. That dark, wet night, in a fierce California rain—they seemed to get it all in one storm—he'd been on an overpass, looking down at another sort of flooding river, an endless river of cars. Shivering, he fought not to give up, not to hurl himself into that stream as the world thought he once had into another deadly river.

He'd actually been straddling the railing, trying to think of one reason not to do it, when he'd heard the squeal of brakes. He came within a hairsbreadth of making the irrevocable decision, before whoever it was who had stopped could stop him.

Then he realized they hadn't stopped for him, but for a bedraggled, soaked-to-the-skin dog, skinny, limping, but moving on. And in that instant he'd felt like less than that dog, who kept moving despite it all, driven by the instinct for life that had once driven him to escape, but now seemed to have deserted him completely.

"Hey! Give me a hand with him, will you? He's hurt."

The voice that had come out of the night had a touch of a drawl, and the man who'd issued the request was tall, lean, with slightly shaggy hair, and while older than he, still young. Although he was dressed in faded jeans, a worn denim shirt and jacket, and oddly, battered cowboy boots, the vehicle was newer, and well kept.

He heard the man talking to the frightened dog, coaxing, crouching down to be at the animal's height. The dog took a tentative step toward the man, stepping into the beam of the headlights.

"He looked like Kula," he said now, not realizing in the swirl of memories that somewhere in his pitiful tale he had begun to talk in almost full sentences. "Same color...but mostly the same eyes. That old soul."

"So you helped," Jessa whispered in a strained voice, the first thing she'd said since he'd slipped back into that nightmare turned salvation.

"Had to. That dog was braver than I was." He took a breath and plowed on; now that he'd started, he knew he had to finish. "Got him loaded in the back of the car. Guy pulled off his jacket, rubbed the dog almost dry." Another memory stabbed him. "There was a blanket. Asked him why he didn't use that. He said...I was going to need it."

He shivered as if it were that cold, wet night all over again.

"He offered me a lift. I didn't have anywhere to go, but...I couldn't get my mind back to what I'd been about to do. And the car would be dry."

She murmured something he couldn't quite understand, but the sound was so full of pain that it didn't matter that he hadn't understood the words. She was, as she always had been, aching for him. That both pained him and thrilled him, in a twisted combination of emotions that he told himself he'd sort out later. Much later, when he was ready to deal with the fact that he was feeling emotions at all.

"I knew—you learn to tell, on the street—he wasn't...one of those. He told me to get in, and I did. I didn't trust anyone, but I couldn't seem to...say no to him." His mouth quirked upward then. "Still can't."

She pulled back again, to look up at him. When she saw his expression, her own changed, lightened.

"Still?"

"He's my boss. Has been since that day."

"You work for him?"

He nodded. "No skills. But I could organize. And track. Plan. Knew some people, some shady, some not. Build a network, he said. Started as his assistant, researcher and general gofer." He gave her a lopsided smile. She smiled back so quickly it warmed him. "Still am. It's just a bigger deal now."

"A bigger deal?"

"Much."

He saw the curiosity come into her eyes, knew she was going to ask, and wondered what her reaction would be when she got the answer.

"Who is he?"

He held her gaze as he spoke the name known around the world.

"Josh Redstone."

Chapter 18

Jessa knew she was having trouble processing it all when the first thing she asked him was, "What happened to the dog?"

"Died."

The cold word jabbed at her, and she winced. Of course the dog had died, he was talking about two decades ago. But that hadn't been what she'd asked, and she knew he knew it. The quickness with which he amended the terse answer proved it.

"Sorry. Years later. In Josh's lap, after the first flight of the Hawk III."

She wanted to smile at the real answer, and the image that presented. Josh Redstone. She had suspected, when she'd heard of Redstone's interest in Riverside Paper, but still, of all the places in the world she could have imagined him ending up had she known he was alive, she doubted that Redstone Incorporated would have occurred to her.

"He just…took you on? You helped him with a stray dog and he hired you on the spot?"

His mouth quirked. "Wouldn't have taken a job. Didn't trust...anybody that much."

"But?"

"But Josh is smart about people. Took me—and the dog—to the hangar he was working out of. Said he had too much work to do to look out for Clover—named him for an old airfield—and asked me to do it. Couldn't pay me, but gave me a bunk there, and meals."

"Josh Redstone couldn't pay you?"

"The Hawk I was still a prototype, then." He was remembering, she could tell by the slightly unfocused look of his eyes. "But later that year she took the light aviation world by storm, and Josh was on top of the world."

"You've been with him ever since?"

"Yes."

"That's a long time."

"Only two people with him longer."

She remembered an article about Josh Redstone her father had given her to read a few years earlier. She'd been in college, and frustrated at the fecklessness of most of her fellow students of the male persuasion. Her father had told her there were other kinds out there, and had handed her the article as proof. She had only scanned it until she got to the part about Redstone being in his twenties when his first design had taken to the air.

"A real man," Jess Hill had said. "Making his own way, not expecting anything to be handed to him, knowing he had to prove himself, prove his design was the best."

Jessa had taken note; her father was a genial, kindly man, but he didn't all that often express such unreserved admiration. She'd read the article carefully, noting that Josh Redstone's life had had its share of lows to go with the highs; he'd lost his wife to cancer, and the article had stated that he'd never remarried.

"And he's a straight shooter," her father had added. "Inspires loyalty, the kind you can't buy with just high salaries."

Her father, as he'd usually been about people, had obviously been right if Josh Redstone had people still with him after that long.

"Who?" she asked, genuinely curious, not simply because she couldn't decide how to ask the rest of what she wanted to know, what he'd done every minute of every day since that awful morning when she'd stood on their rock and stared at the river that had always been a silent companion but then had turned enemy.

"Draven. John. Head of security." She remembered a mention of that, as well, that Redstone Security was a legend in itself, earning respect, admiration and sometimes envy around the world as it worked to protect Redstone and the Redstone family. "Served with Josh's brother in the army. With him when he died. Came to tell Josh, never left."

Beneath her empathy for the story he was telling, she was aware he was being, for him, positively expansive. She seized the mood, thinking that he could clam up anew at any moment.

"And the third?"

"Tess Machado. First pilot he hired. No one else would—she was just a kid, and a woman. Josh saw her land a flight school plane with a collapsed nose gear perfectly in a crosswind that should have made it impossible. Hired her on the spot."

Jessa felt a moment's pleasure that one of Josh Redstone's first people was a woman, mixed with deepening curiosity about the man who saw what others had missed.

As he had with this man, even as a boy.

"The triumvirate," St. John said softly.

"Draven, Tess...and you?"

He nodded. "Mac labeled us."

"Mac?"

"Harlen McClaren. Our honorary fourth. Doesn't really work at Redstone, but he gave Josh the kick start."

The moment he spoke the name of the famous treasure hunter, she remembered the bit in that article she'd read, that

McClaren had invested in Redstone when it was nothing but a hangar and a dream.

"We were there when Elizabeth died," he said, his voice tight. "We thought it would destroy him. We were all afraid. Took turns sitting with him, dogging him, nagging him, until he came out of the tunnel."

It struck her hard, that parallel to her own life now, and her mother. And his expression told her he knew it, and she realized he'd meant it to give her hope.

And it had.

"So…what is it you do at Redstone?"

"Told you."

She had a feeling there was a bit more to it by now than general gofer. Something faintly amused in his expression told her she was right. But she let it go for the moment.

"Where do you live?"

"Redstone Headquarters."

She chuckled. "I've heard he inspires that kind of dedication, but—" She broke off as she looked at him. "Wait. You meant that…literally?"

He nodded. "Top floor. Apartment. Like to stay close. Monitor things."

"There are apartments in Redstone Headquarters?"

"Three. Mine. Josh's, for when he's jammed. Third for whoever needs it."

That alone told her he was far from just a gofer; if he rated a permanent apartment at Redstone Headquarters, if Josh Redstone wanted him close by to monitor things, he was much more.

"Whoever?" she asked.

"Redstone," he said, "takes care of our own."

That, too, had been one of the main points of the article, that the entire massive power of Redstone would be mobilized for the lowest echelon of their people, if necessary. The Redstone family was just that. But she was too focused on the way he said "our own" to give it more than a passing thought. The

Redstone family, she thought again. He was part of it. And she felt a burst of grateful warmth that he'd landed there, found some kind of family at last.

…the entire massive power of Redstone.

Her own thought came back to her, and belatedly the pieces tumbled into place.

This was how he'd done it. The bank, the investigative reporter, the sudden interest of a global giant like Redstone in a company in this rural, un-noteworthy place.

"You are going to destroy him," she whispered. "You're going to use Redstone to grind him up."

This time it was he who echoed her. "Problem?"

"No. No one deserves it more. I'm just…a little in awe." And at finding out battered, tortured Adam Alden had not only landed on his feet, but obviously done so with considerable success. "I mean…Redstone."

He smiled then, and it was the closest to a natural, normal smile she'd seen since he'd come back. "Yes. Redstone."

"Is it…everything I've heard?"

"And more."

"What's he like?"

"Everything you'd hope." He gave her a sideways look. "Some ways, like your father."

She smiled in turn at that. "He admired him. But Dad was happy to stay here, in little Cedar. Josh Redstone built an empire."

"Yes. And fought off those who want to destroy it." His expression darkened. "So far," he muttered, as if to himself.

Jessa couldn't imagine why anyone would want to destroy something as magnificent as Redstone. "Competitors?"

St. John laughed, harshly. "Can't compete. So clear the field. Sound familiar?"

The tactics did sound too familiar. "Your father."

"Yes."

She had nothing more to say to the stark truth of that. The computer monitor flashed as the bot left on another search.

She'd have to adjust that, she thought. Once or twice a day would be enough, every hour was overkill. She smiled wryly as she realized she was making plans on how to use this system she couldn't afford and was already loath to give up. She had—

Another realization interrupted her own thoughts.

She had had a Redstone exec, or whatever he was, doing computer grunt work, apparently all night, in her little feed and hardware store.

"This," she said, gesturing at the new setup, "this is from Redstone?"

"Been building our own for a while now," he said. "Barton does the geek work. He's a genius. Could have his own department, but loves working for Gamble."

Gamble. She remembered Uncle Larry mentioning the name. Ian Gamble, that oddity in this day and age, one man who invented. Brilliantly. The article had talked of all those who had tried to lure him away from Redstone, but he'd laughed in their faces. Even the government had come calling, but he wouldn't speak to them at all. Josh Redstone had given him a chance when no one else would, gave him the kind of free rein he would never find anywhere else, he'd told the interviewer. He would stay with Redstone until he died or Josh closed the doors.

"And just how much would last night's work cost, at what Redstone pays you?"

He shrugged.

"I don't take charity," she said.

He met her gaze then. And for an instant, the usually cool, steady gaze seemed to soften. "Not. You paid me long ago."

Emotion welled up inside her, a confusing tangle of the old ache and a new one she hadn't yet dared to put a name to.

With uncharacteristic avoidance she dodged thinking about that. She told herself she simply wasn't ready to face that snarl in her already complicated life just now. And as she dodged those thoughts, she ran smack into another. And this one she couldn't dodge, if for no other reason than she had once before, and had never forgiven herself.

"Tyler," she said.

He went still.

"He's where you were. He's in that same hell."

"When he goes down, kid will be free."

"If he lives that long," Jessa said, reaching out and grabbing his hands. "He's not as strong as you were, and I don't think as smart."

He shook his head sharply, she wasn't sure at exactly what.

"You learned. You figured out how to dodge your father, how to anticipate, to stay clear, and he *still* nearly destroyed you."

She felt the shiver that went through him then, knew she was reaching him.

"Dam," she said, using his adopted name for the first time, "Tyler's trapped, just like you were. Abandoned, betrayed by those who should love and protect him."

He still didn't speak. Jessa knew she would never have a better chance to break through his single-minded determination.

"I've met his mother. She's as blind, or as weak as yours was. She'll just stand by and let it happen, out of fear or, damn it, because she doesn't want to lose what she has."

She heard a sound from him then, an odd sort of strained choking, as if he were fighting down an eruption of words.

"Your plan," she said softly, "it's working. It's getting to him. It's making him angry enough to lose his cool in public, and people are seeing it. They're rethinking. He might even lose this election. But who's paying the real price?"

"Have to stop him." The words came out from behind clenched teeth.

"Yes. I know that. You know I know that, or I wouldn't be doing this in the first place. But Tyler…"

He shuddered this time, she felt it through his hands, still slack under hers.

"We have to help him," she whispered. "We can't leave him alone, helpless, bewildered by things that are so hideous they shouldn't, can't be borne. There are agencies, people to help, more than there were when…"

Her voice trailed off. He was looking at the floor, but she knew he wasn't seeing the old, scarred wood.

"He's your stepbrother," she said. "I know you don't know him, and it probably means less than nothing, after what you've been through, but…*I* can't leave him to that. I didn't do anything when I should have, once. It's been hard enough living with that. It torments me every single day. I couldn't live with myself if I did it again."

He looked at her then. In the same instant his hands came alive under hers, gripping her fingers and pulling her closer.

He said nothing, simply pulled her into his arms, into an embrace she didn't even think about resisting. She wrapped her arms around him, holding him, wishing that by some magic she could erase it all for him. All the vicious, ugly memories, all the pain, the agony of betrayal, she wished she could take it away.

She couldn't. Nothing could.

But he let her hold him. And for now, in this moment, it was enough.

Chapter 19

His stepbrother.

St. John stared at the boy who was sitting on a bench on the sidelines of the early-evening soccer practice, his left arm in a cast, his left eye still swollen nearly shut. It would, he knew, turn black soon and take weeks to completely fade. He wondered if the boy looked in the mirror and saw it as the price he'd paid for not being quick enough or smart enough to avoid it. He wondered if the boy resolved to be better, to behave perfectly, only to discover it made no difference. He wondered if the boy had begun to make intricate plans to avoid contact at all with his tormenter.

He wondered if the boy spent hours trying to figure out what it was about him that made Albert Alden hate him.

Slowly he walked over to the bench. Calculating what the boy would think a safe distance, he sat down just more than an arm's reach away. Tyler gave him a sideways glance, although he didn't meet his eyes. It was as if he'd just wanted to reassure himself whoever this person was, he wasn't close enough to be a danger.

He was wary, skittish, but he hadn't learned yet, St. John thought. Hadn't learned that with some predators, no distance was enough, there was no safety to be found anywhere with them, except in death.

If he stayed here, he would learn.

If he didn't figure out the nature of his enemy quickly, he would learn sooner.

If St. John kept pushing Alden, kept tightening the vise he'd set in motion, it might be the last thing he ever learned.

He knew what the boy was feeling. Just as he'd known when he'd been a kid just a couple of years older than Tyler, that if he didn't escape, he would die. The idea of heading off into nowhere, where he knew nothing and no one, had been terrifying. The idea of dying had been more terrifying. And in no small part because it had begun to seem tempting. And he'd begun to understand why his mother had felt it her only choice.

He shook off the memories and focused on the boy sitting on the bench, alone and apart, as he had so often been. He had the feeling this was going to be futile. He'd never dealt well with kids. Josh said it was because he'd never really had the chance to be one himself.

He knew that commenting on the boy's injuries would be the wrong approach; nothing had been worse than constantly having to lie about what had happened, to keep his ugly secret.

"Rather be playing?" he said at last.

After a moment's hesitation, and still with no eye contact, Tyler said bluntly, "No."

"Why not?"

"No good."

"That's why they call it practice."

"Don't want me."

St. John fell silent. The boy had spoken all of a half dozen words, yet he had revealed so much. And the irony that it was himself speaking in full sentences to the boy's terse answers wasn't lost on him.

The beating-down process, the sense of worthlessness, was well on its way. And the isolation, the apartness was there, as well; whether it was by choice or because the kids around him knew he was different in ways they didn't want to know about didn't really matter. He felt an ache rising inside him, a pain he'd never thought he'd feel again. But looking at this boy was like looking at himself, all those years ago, and the thought of what pure hell was yet to come made his gut knot almost unbearably.

Tyler said nothing more. So he'd already begun to learn what St. John had early on; the less you talked, the less attention you drew to yourself. In the beginning, he'd tried to limit that to just his father, but it had been too hard to make the switch back and forth, so he'd resorted to the minimum of words with everyone—everyone except Jessa. She'd been the only one he could relax his guard around.

The rest of the world got that surly, near-silence. It had earned him the reputation he had today, but it had, on occasion, saved him, so he considered it worth it.

He talks like he's at war....

He'd heard it said around Redstone, knew it had originated with Gabe Taggert, the former naval officer who was now captain of Redstone's flagship, Josh's latest venture into nautical design.

He'd also heard that Gabe's wife Cara's response had been simply, "Maybe he is."

That's what this was. The final battle of a war that had been interrupted by the retreat of the weaker adversary. But he'd learned, he'd gotten stronger, he'd gathered the weapons, although he'd never intended to use them like this. Had his father stayed off his radar, he wouldn't be here.

And he never would have seen Jess again.

The jolt that gave him was beyond unsettling.

"You're Jessa's friend, aren't you?"

For an instant it seemed as if the boy had read his mind, and it took him a moment to answer.

"Yes."

"I like her."

"So do I." And that, he thought, was an understatement if ever there'd been one.

"And Maui."

"He likes you, too."

The boy's expression brightened. "Really?"

St. John nodded. And then Tyler looked away, drawing back into himself in a way he knew all too well.

"Don't tell," the boy whispered.

"Tell what?" St. John asked.

"About Maui."

"Tell who?"

The boy didn't answer, but the fear in the gaze that darted his way and then dodged away told him.

"Something might happen to him." The boy slid off the bench, cradling his broken arm with the other. "Gotta go."

St. John watched him go, with a wrenching sadness he couldn't fight. A cheer went up from the soccer field, seeming miles away rather than just a few yards. And a world away from the life Tyler Alden was living.

St. John left the park, walking toward town, glad now he'd left his rental parked at Hill's. He needed the exertion. He'd be running if he didn't know it would earn him, in street clothes, attention he didn't want. And that realization shook him; where was the vaunted St. John control? Where was the legendary cool, the emotionless assessment of every situation?

The more complicated the plan, the bigger the chance for failure.

That had always been his philosophy, even when it came to the biggest of ventures for Redstone. And he'd applied it here; the plan was simple—drive Alden to expose his true self—it was only the execution that had been a bit complicated. And it was working, just as he'd known it would. The smooth, polished facade was cracking, giving glimpses of the ugly, twisted soul beneath. And soon—sooner than he'd even thought—that crack would become an irreversible breach, and Albert Alden's life as he knew it would be over.

But now he had to face the very real possibility that the self-destruction he'd engineered for a man who deserved every iota of it might also destroy the life of an innocent boy, trapped as he once had been. Destroy it in a brutal, very literal sense.

He consciously slowed his steps as he realized he was on the verge of breaking into that run.

And clenched his jaw against the turmoil raging inside him when he realized that he wasn't hurrying to get back to his car.

He was hurrying to get to Jessa.

She had always been the one clean, pure, golden thing in his life.

It seemed she still was.

Chapter 20

"He likes you."

At his words, Jessa looked at St. John as he paced the space near the hay bales in the storage barn. She heard a round of applause from the square, where Alden was holding another rally. Maybe it was her imagination, but it didn't seem as loud as it had been in the past. Or as frequent. And the rumble of dissent was actually heard now and then, unlike before.

People were getting curious. Several had approached her, asking about his public explosion. She told them the truth, but she no longer felt the sense of pride she initially had in how she'd handled it. She couldn't, not when it had cost Tyler so dearly.

Which brought her back to the matter at hand.

"I think he likes Maui more," Jessa said, reaching down to tickle the dog's ears. The animal lifted his head obligingly, leaning into her caress.

"Talks to you."

"He talked to you, too."

"Not much."

"By your standards, that would mean total silence," Jessa said drily.

Usually a retort like that had earned her, if nothing else, a quirk of his mouth. This time all he did was keep staring out the window at…well, she wasn't sure what. But she was pretty sure it wasn't the physical reality outside.

"Too late to stop it all."

She went very still. She hadn't expected him to reach this point so quickly. She hadn't even been sure he would reach it at all.

"Stop it?"

"Can call off Redstone. The audit, the reporter, no."

"Is that what you want? To stop it?" That he would even consider it startled her.

"Kid will end up dead."

"Like you almost did," she said, then held her breath.

"My revenge. In a way, his. But—" He shook his head, then went on in a low, harsh voice, "Unacceptable loss."

Jessa couldn't begin to describe the relief that filled her. Since the moment she'd realized who he was, and had watched his inexorable march toward that well-deserved revenge, she had wondered. Had wondered if the damage done to him as a child had twisted him into something as cold and calculating as his father. There had been times when she'd thought it true as she watched his fierce, intense focus on bringing the man down.

But here was the truth, the real man. The man who realized he couldn't sacrifice an innocent boy trapped just as he had been, to this cause, no matter how righteous.

"I talked to his mother," Jessa said. St. John's head moved sharply as his gaze shot to her face. "She's not going to be any help. I'd guess Alden has managed to restrain himself from venting his sick proclivities on her, and she's either in total denial about her son, or worse, has decided better him than her. Disgusting as it is, I think it's the latter."

St. John was staring at her, not speaking, and in that moment she knew just what he was thinking about.

"It doesn't make your mother's path any more acceptable, she still should have fought for you, but it does make it seem... almost cleaner, doesn't it?"

"You'd fight." It was barely above a whisper.

"For my child? To the death. Or his abuser's death," she added, meaning it with all her heart. "What are we going to do? If Alden cracks—"

"When."

"All right, when. You know him better than anyone, so if you say he will, he will. But what do we do about Tyler? How do we keep him safe? If I call the child welfare people, it's going to look like I'm just trying to smear him, and they might not take it seriously enough to move in time. And if you call, you'll have to answer questions you don't want to answer."

"School," he said.

"Like they did for you? The man bought them that damned soccer field, they named it after him." She couldn't keep the fury she was feeling from creeping into her voice. "They're going to need a lot more than a political opponent's say-so to take any action against him. A lot of the teachers are out campaigning for him."

"Payback."

"Maybe. The reason doesn't really matter, though. What matters is Tyler."

"Give him...somewhere to run to."

"How?"

He glanced at Maui, whose plumed golden tail wagged at the eye contact alone. And she remembered the story he'd told her, about how a scared, exhausted boy on the verge of ending it all had come back from the brink...to help a man with a dog.

"Use Maui?" His gaze shifted back to her face, and she read the question there. "All right. Tyler's safety is paramount. And Maui certainly won't mind. But how?"

"Trust you."

Her brow furrowed. Sometimes, she thought with a touch of exasperation. "Do you mean you trust me to figure something out, or that Tyler will trust me?"

For an instant something brighter flashed in his eyes, something less haunted. Then, quietly, almost solemnly, even for him, he spoke one word.

"Yes."

She couldn't help it, despite the gravity of the situation and the nature of the discussion, she smiled.

"Well, he'd likely trust Maui, anyway."

"You. I did."

A bittersweet warmth flooded her. "And I let you down," she whispered.

For the first time since he'd come back utter horror registered on his face, echoed in his voice. "Jess, no!"

He crossed the six feet between them in two long strides. Abruptly, without gentleness or finesse, he yanked her against him and wrapped his arms around her.

"Don't think that. Don't ever. You were…all I had."

She stood with her face against his chest, her ear pressed so close she could hear the rumble of the words over the hammering of his heart.

"Should have told someone," she insisted.

"You were a kid."

She let out a shivering sigh. "I'm an honest person, I try to do the right thing…so how, twice in my life, did I end up in a place where I know something horrible but can't tell because no one would believe me?"

"Common denominator."

She blinked, and although she was loath to surrender the close contact, pulled back to look up at him.

"What?"

"Common denominator. Who?"

"Me," she said, puzzled.

To her surprise, he smiled, but it was an oddly pained smile.

"Figures. Blame yourself first. Like you." Then he shook his head. "Not you. Him."

"Oh."

She lowered her head to his chest again, unwilling to give up the closeness as she processed what he'd said. And realized she couldn't deny he was right. And that it made her feel better to realize that perhaps it wasn't her that attracted some cosmic weirdness that had twice put her in this position, that it was Alden and his consistent evil.

She heard his heartbeat suddenly speed up in the same moment a low sound escaped him. She looked up at him then, caught him staring down at her with a hot, intense gleam that made his eyes seem darker. Or maybe it was just the shadow from the brim of that old-fashioned cap.

An image shot through her mind then of an old photograph her father had once shown her of Clark Alden. The man who had made the Alden fortune, the clever entrepreneur who had stayed in Cedar when he could have gone anywhere, and who had kept the little town going even as others died away from lack of industry or business.

In that photograph, the man had been wearing a suit from another era, the stiff, stern expression that seemed required in photographs of that age, and…that cap. Adam had left his world behind, but he'd taken that cap, a symbol of the one man who had been on his side.

So many emotions welled up in her that she could hardly contain them. She reached up, brushed her fingers over his jaw, tracing the new scar, the mark of his escape, with a gentle touch.

She heard him suck in a breath.

"Jess," he said, in a harsh, grating whisper that sounded on the edge of agony.

Her breath caught in her throat.

She froze, not daring to move, to make a sound, nothing that might make him change his mind. She realized she'd been waiting for this from the moment she'd realized who he really was. Probably even before; from the moment she'd first seen him.

And then his mouth was on hers, fierce, demanding; no tender, tentative first kiss this, but a declaration of a need so great it snapped all tethers in the first moment his lips pressed against hers.

In that instant the calm, usually serene person she was vanished, to be replaced by some wild creature she didn't recognize. Something huge and starbright burst inside her as he deepened the kiss with an urgency that told her whatever crazed madness had seized her had seized him, as well.

She felt another shock as his tongue swept past her lips, probing, demanding, and an even bigger shock as she surrendered, willingly, wanting more, more and still more. Her fingers dug into his shoulders as she hung on, as if he were the only solid thing in her suddenly spinning world.

She realized vaguely she was pressed against him from chest to thigh, realized he was completely, thoroughly aroused. Nothing in her experience had prepared her for this, because she'd never felt anything like this, hadn't known this kind of all-consuming need actually existed.

"Dam," she whispered, and left it at that; whether he interpreted it as his name or an oath didn't matter, either one would be equally heartfelt.

"Close the store." It came in that same harsh whisper.

"Yes," she said, knowing she was saying yes to much more than simply closing the store an hour early.

Moments later, in his car, headed the back way out of Cedar, avoiding the crowd in the square, Jessa wondered if along the way she would regain her senses and put a halt to what she knew was about to happen.

And answered her own question when she realized she'd started down this road a very long time ago.

"I always wanted you to be the first."

St. John went still, frozen by her quiet words, the first she'd spoken since that whispered "Yes," that had sent every system in his body into overdrive.

"I didn't even think about it until years after you were gone. And I didn't know exactly what it was I was wanting, then, but later, in college…when it was my first time, I understood. I was sad that it wasn't you."

He stared at her, standing there in the motel room that had seemed more than adequate for himself, but now seemed far too shabby for her. It wasn't shabby at all, he knew, it was simply her golden, pure beauty that made it seem so to him.

Oddly, her quiet, almost shy admission served to do what nothing else had been able to; he got a grip on his reeling senses.

"Jess…if you don't want…"

The smile that curved her mouth then stopped him short. "Only you," she said with a tinge of humor in her soft voice, "could read that into what I said. I want, Dameron St. John," she said, as if she were using the full name to emphasize that she knew she was no longer dealing with the boy she'd once known. "I didn't get what I wanted then. So are you going to take this away from me, too? What I've been waiting all my adult life for?"

And so, he realized with a jolt that shook him nearly to the bone, had he. Not that there hadn't been women along the way, women who understood his limitations, who were willing to indulge without expecting anything more than what transpired in those few moments that should have been intimate but were, in fact, businesslike.

But this was Jessa, and all bets were off. If she had any sense, she'd walk out of here right now, while he could let her do it. If he had any sense, he'd take her back to Cedar and deposit her safely on her mother's doorstep. What the hell did he think he was doing?

She frowned suddenly, and he wondered if her good sense had recovered.

"Speaking of adult," she said, "I don't make a habit of carrying condoms around."

Of course she didn't. "Not an issue," he said gruffly. "Tests every six months. Insurance."

She gave him an odd look. "I wasn't thinking of STDs," she said. "I was thinking of babies."

Something bitter and sharp-edged sliced through him, something he hadn't known was living buried deep inside him. He had, incredibly, forgotten. It had never been a concern in his life.

"Not an issue," he said again, his voice sounding like a bad gravel road even to him.

She lifted a brow at him.

"Vasectomy. Years ago."

He saw the realization dawn in her eyes, saw that she knew exactly why he'd done it, understood why he could never risk having children.

He'd never in his life expected to regret it.

"Change your mind?"

He had to ask it, even as he hated doing it, fearing her answer would be yes.

"My hopes, maybe. My mind...no."

Before he could interpret what she'd meant by that, she was kissing him. Willingly, reaching up, pressing herself against him.

Part of his mind was screaming that this was too much, too big, that if he took this step it was irrevocable. That the change it would bring was irrevocable.

At the same time he knew there was no way he could resist; this was Jess, and he'd lost the power to say no to her. If he'd ever had it.

Her mouth on his was destroying the walls he'd built so thick and so high, keeping him apart. The vaunted St. John cool was shattered, destroyed by the realization that this bright, vibrant spirit wanted him. She knew everything, she always had, and she still wanted him.

He knew he had only moments before he lost it completely. He threw every mental barrier he had left against the one thing that must never be allowed to touch her. It left everything else open, bare to her, but he didn't care.

He felt her pull back. Protest rose in the back of his throat. But then she reached down to grab the hem of her sweater and pulled it up over her head. His breath left him in a gasp as his gaze hungrily took in the soft, feminine curves of hips above low-slung jeans, and the enticing, luscious swell of breasts nestled into a pale blue bra.

"Please," she whispered. "Don't stop now."

And a few desperate, fumbling moments later, when he was as bare to her literally as figuratively, he knew deep in his soul this was his last, best chance to truly exorcise the demon.

Naked, they went down to the bed locked together. He'd spent his life being the planner, the information center, taking the skills inadvertently taught to him by his father and making them work in other ways. But no plan he could ever have made could have prepared him for this. Because he hadn't known this, this kind of heat, building to conflagration even existed.

And then she was touching him, her hands sliding over his bare skin, searching, stroking, as if she wanted to memorize him. He understood the need; he traced the lines of her, the long, soft curves, not caring if she noticed his hands were shaking. It was safe with her, everything he was and had been was safe with her, he knew that with a gut-deep certainty he'd never felt before—except in a sun-touched meadow by a river years ago. And it struck him that this was the day they should have eventually had, had his life been normal, that someday, when the four years between them wouldn't have made any difference, they would have discovered this fiery heaven together.

I always wanted you to be the first....

He groaned, shuddering as she slid one hand down his belly, found and stroked his rigid flesh, sending a shock wave through him that made him shudder down to his toes and tightened every muscle in his body. He cupped her breasts, shuddering anew at the way her nipples tightened at the first brush of his thumbs, and at the soft moan that escaped her.

"Dam," she whispered, and something in her voice made him lift his head and look at her. The fierce heat that was engulfing him was echoed in her eyes, but there was concern there, too. Through the fog of pleasure it took him a moment to realize what it was. When he did, the answer to her unspoken question was as powerful as the need that gripped him.

"He's not here. He never will be. Not with us."

It came out like a growl, but he knew she would understand. This was Jessa, and she always understood.

She moved then, arching against him, pressing her breasts against his hands. He lifted, lowered his mouth to them, flicked her nipples with his tongue, savoring the gasping cry that broke from her.

And that cry broke him. He couldn't touch enough, kiss enough, move fast enough. He was out of his mind and knew it, but it didn't matter, because it was Jess, and she had always been the help he needed to keep the demon at bay.

When at last she urged him with a moaned plea, and he slid into her slick heat, he shuddered at the sweet, bone-deep pleasure of it. He began to move, and the heat built, friction and grasp, wet and slide, and he knew he was too close, it was going too fast, tried to slow down, but her hands were all over him, her mouth seeking, kissing, licking, and there was nothing in the world but this place and this moment. When she cried out his name and he felt her body clench around his, he let loose the last restraint, knowing the demon was helpless now, destroyed by the pure heart of this woman.

"Jess!"

It burst from him as his body responded to the sweet grip of hers, the ripples of her muscles coaxing him over the edge into a free fall unlike anything he'd ever known. It was an insane sort of wildness that ripped through barriers he'd thought impervious.

He'd been wrong. Again.

And much later, he knew that the sordid memories he had once attached to this kind of intimacy would never escape their cage again. In the face of this kind of pure joy they didn't have a chance. They would always be there, but they were locked up for good now, no match for the fierceness and determination of the woman in his arms.

Chapter 21

Jess felt as if she'd at long last completed a picture she'd begun to paint years ago. It couldn't have been finished before, but was no less beautiful for the delay. Her body still hummed with the pleasure of it, and while she might never have known what she was missing had he not come back, she'd always known it would be best with him.

She'd been right.

And it was an afternoon she would never, ever forget. They'd run the gamut in those three hours, from the frantic need of the first time, to a more normal urgency, and then to a slower, gentler pace, when he'd rolled them over while still inside her, giving her control, a gift she'd only later realized the full significance of.

Just as she'd only realized the other ramifications as they drove back into Cedar and she'd seen one of her own campaign signs.

"Well," she'd muttered, "wouldn't the busybodies in town just love to find out what this candidate's been up to?"

"Don't let them."

She glanced at him then, as she hadn't dared to since they'd gotten into his rental car, because every time she looked at him her body reacted so fiercely it was almost embarrassing.

"I'm not sure it's not emblazoned on my forehead."

To her surprise a smile flickered on his face for a moment. He didn't look at her, and she wondered if he was experiencing the same reaction she was having.

"Really a problem?" he asked.

"Could be," she said honestly. "Cedar is still a small town, and I'm the good girl. Not supposed to be off doing..."

"Me?" he suggested when her voice trailed off.

"Anyone," she said, although the tiny ring of humor in his voice had her smiling inwardly. "But if they knew, and knew who you really are..."

After a moment he nodded, and she knew he'd realized what she meant.

"And don't think I don't see the irony," she said wryly. "Honest, wonderful, consenting-adult sex could lose me the election to a too-twisted-to-live pervert."

"Wonderful?" he said after a moment.

It was so normal, such a normal guy reaction, that she nearly laughed at the sudden burst of joy that filled her. "Beyond wonderful. Beyond my wildest dreams. But it wasn't a surprise. I knew it would be like this, with you."

"Didn't know it *could* be. With anyone."

The muttered words weren't a declaration of love, but coming from him, they might as well have been.

And for the first time Jessa let herself hope that they had a chance to leave the past behind, except for the memories worth keeping.

A chance was all she wanted.

Jessa watched the boy and the dog, thinking it would be a joyous slice of Americana if the situation weren't so dire. Tyler could still throw a ball with his right arm, and had been doing so delightedly for nearly fifteen minutes now, the tireless Maui finding it wherever it landed, frequently leaping over the big log that lay crossways in the middle of the yard, and romping back with it in an irresistible invitation to keep the game going.

"Try a fly ball, Tyler," Jessa called to him. "But let him know first. Just wave the ball and say 'up.'"

The boy gave an excited nod, and did as instructed. Maui's body language immediately changed, and he backed off a few feet, eyes glued to the grubby ball the boy held. Tyler tossed it skyward. Maui positioned himself with the skill of an all-star right fielder, then launched himself in the same direction, catching the descending ball neatly in midair.

An excited yell broke from Tyler. Jessa smiled. And chided herself for not having done this long ago. She should have realized Tyler would need a haven, and provided it. It was simply the right thing to do.

It had been easy enough to learn what days Alden would be in River Mill by checking the hours posted at his office there. Over the past week she had made certain she—and Maui—were within the boy's sight in the afternoons after school, and the urge of boy toward dog had done the rest. And she knew it wasn't her imagination that the boy looked a bit less beaten down, acted a bit less skittish, at least around her and Maui.

The task she'd set herself had had another benefit as, needing the time for this, she had turned to her mother for help in the store. Her mother had responded as if she'd only needed a reason, and had come in to cover for her on these days. And to Jessa's surprise, her mother had also taken to the new computer system with a surprising interest, learning quickly and not taking the least offense that this modernization her husband had always resisted had been done.

"It only makes sense," she'd told her startled daughter. "And," she added with a look that had made Jessa wonder if the huge change in her life wasn't stamped across her forehead in neon ink, "it was remarkably generous of your Mr. St. John to do all this."

It was Maui's sudden veering off his track that warned her. The dog yelped happily and, ball still in his mouth, made a sharp right turn. And Jessa knew when she turned, she would see St. John approaching, as they'd planned.

They'd waited until Tyler had relaxed a bit, had gotten used to things. And while when the boy spotted St. John a wariness came over him, he didn't run. Especially when Maui, after a bouncing greeting to St. John, came back to him to resume the game.

"Great dog," St. John said, looking at the boy.

Tyler nodded, still wary.

"You remember my…friend?" Jessa asked Tyler, stumbling awkwardly over what exactly to call him, then choosing the easiest thing for a child. St. John gave her a look that told her he understood her hesitation perfectly, but agreed this was not the time to discuss exactly what he was to her.

Tyler nodded, giving St. John a furtive glance. "Don't know your name, though."

"St. John," he said. Then, as if realizing that was a bit off for the boy to use, he said, sounding awkward in turn, "First name's Dameron. Dam, for short."

The boy blinked. "That's a bad word."

She saw St. John take a deep breath. She'd warned him the boy wasn't going to be able to follow his cryptic conversational leaps, that real sentences were going to be necessary here.

"Do you think like you talk?" she'd asked him last night, when they'd decided today was the day he'd approach Tyler. "Is it in your mind like that, like machine-gun fire?"

"No."

He'd smiled, as if he realized the humor of the one-word answer to that question, and pulled her closer against him. She'd snuggled into his warmth in the twilight that came through the window of his room.

"Yes. I chose it," St. John said now, in answer to the boy's wide-eyed statement, "because my father always told me I was bad."

Tyler blinked. "He did?"

"He told me I was stupid, disobedient and most of all not worthy of him, so I had to be punished."

Tyler went pale. And very, very still. Jessa could read in his shocked eyes that Alden hadn't changed his approach in the last two decades, that these were words this small boy had heard before, and often. Probably the exact words, if his stunned expression was anything to go by. Maui seemed to sense the change in mood, and dropped the ball, understanding the game was over.

"He used to do that to me," St. John said, nodding at the cast on the boy's arm. "And that," he went on, reaching out and not quite touching the boy's face near his now black-and-purple eyes. Tyler flinched, pulled back as if he'd made contact, but he didn't run. Instead, his gaze was fastened on St. John with an intensity that mirrored, Jessa realized, St. John's own.

She stepped back a few steps, until she was out of earshot, giving them the privacy the ugly subject needed. At her quiet finger snap Maui came to her side. She sat down on the fallen log, and the dog gave her a quick, tongue-swiping kiss before settling at her feet and turning his attention back to the man and the boy.

They were sitting on the grass now, and even from here she could see Tyler's occasional shivers. She couldn't hear what St. John was saying to him, and was childishly thankful for that; her imaginings had been bad enough, she didn't want to listen to the details of the reality of what had happened to him. Yet she knew that would be what he would have to use to get through to the boy.

And she knew that he'd known it, from the moment they'd hatched this plan. He would confront his own demons for the sake of a boy he didn't even know. And that told her everything she needed to know about the kind of man he'd become.

"I think he'll come to us."

He spoke after long, sated minutes of silence as they lay together in the fading afternoon light. In the place he'd never been but always tried to picture in his mind; Jessa's room. Although she'd told him this hadn't been her room then. When she'd come home after her father's diagnosis, she'd moved into the large attic that ran the length of the house, to accommodate the things she'd acquired since she'd left home.

She'd arranged it cleverly, using the furniture to divide the big, oblong space into three areas: a desk and bookshelf area at one end, living in the middle, and a bedroom at the other end. A small bathroom had been added in one corner, making the suite comfortable and convenient. She'd used cool colors of green and blue in stripes and blocks in the bedding and curtains at the big windows at each end of the room, and a big area rug in matching tones covered a large expanse of the polished wood floor. Maui's bed was on the floor, but St. John guessed from a couple of stray hairs he'd noticed on the blue comforter that the big dog spent most nights exactly where any male would want to be.

And he never in his life would have expected to end up here himself.

"Yes. You got through to him," Jessa said quietly.

She was curled up against him, her head on his shoulder, one hand lying on his chest. They were the first words she'd spoken since she'd urgently asked him to hurry in helping her rid herself of her clothes. Not that she'd been silent, not at all; his little blond pixie was a vocal lover, albeit not in words. And the sounds she made, and the way she trembled at his touch, nearly drove him mad.

To his own utter shock, it was he who had talked. He who had somehow found the words to string together to tell her how she made him feel. She'd brought him to life in a way he'd never thought possible. He'd long ago given up on ever feeling like this, and the fact that everyone around him at Redstone seemed to have found this kind of sweet madness hadn't made him change his expectations.

"He will," she said when he didn't speak, and he told himself he was grateful she didn't seem to require sweet nothings whispered in her ear, because he was sure he'd make a mess of that. Talking when he was driven to near madness with need for her was one thing, talking like a normal man in the exhausted aftermath of the most incredibly sweet experience of his life was something else.

St. John hoped she was right about Tyler. It had been one of the most difficult things he'd ever done, but he wasn't used to failing at difficult things, and he most especially didn't want to fail at this one. It had been wrenching, gut-twisting, to look at Tyler Alden and see himself. To see himself in the fear and betrayal reflected in the boy's eyes. To see that fear turn to terror when he'd realized his stepfather was due home any moment, and they—and Maui—were still there.

They'd left quickly, reassuring the boy that they could handle his father, that they knew the nature of the enemy. St. John hadn't told Tyler the final truth, that their enemies were indeed the same man, but he'd figured the boy had had enough for one day. Just knowing there was another kindred soul who understood was enough to process.

And now he knew. St. John had wondered if he could do it. But the moment he'd looked into Tyler's haunted eyes, he knew he had to. There was no other option that would leave him able to sleep at night.

Besides, Jessa had asked him to. And that alone, to his amazement, would have been enough. Not just to make the effort to reach Tyler, but to do…just about anything.

Jessa. He drew in a shuddering breath. She shifted, sliding one long, silken leg over him, and he nearly gasped at the simple movement, and the shudder of sensation it sent through him.

They'd stolen these moments together before going back to the store. When they'd left Tyler, she had looked at him with an intensity and admiration that made him think he would literally die if he didn't have her in the next moment. He'd grabbed her shoulders, stared down at her.

"Need you. Now."

To his shock she'd said only, "Mom's at the store. She'll stay there until I come back. The house is empty."

Questions had occurred to him, but were blasted out of his mind before he could ask by the fierce, almost violent reaction of a demanding body.

But now the main, the only real question hovered.

Jessa had been his salvation as a boy, he'd never denied that, never could. The memories were too precious, too clear. But the reality, here in his arms now, her naked body pressed against his, was even more precious, because it was so unexpected. And on some gut level he knew with a certainty that stunned him that she could be his salvation now.

If he wanted it.

Did he? He'd held himself apart for so long, used everything at hand, his ability to intimidate, his dark scowl, and the trademark way of talking—or not talking—to keep the world at a distance. Could he change that now? Did he even want to?

He lay still, betraying nothing of the battle raging in his mind. He had the odd thought that this must be what someone awakening from a coma felt like, bombarded with long unfelt sensations and thoughts, and reeling under the impact.

And his self-imposed coma had been nearly two decades long.

And then Jessa moved again, this time sliding her hand down from his chest until her palm lay flat on his belly. She was only exerting the slightest pressure, yet he felt as if every ounce of blood in his body was rushing to the site of her touch, as if that one point of contact was the only thing connecting him to…anything.

"I don't know how to do this, Jess," he whispered, the words ripped from somewhere so deep inside him he thought they must have left a bloody trail on their way to his lips.

For a moment she was silent, then she raised herself up on one elbow and looked at him.

"I'll forgo the obvious retort to that, because I know that's not what you mean. But just for the record, you certainly know how to do *part* of this, and magnificently well, thank you."

Her voice was deadly serious, but there was a glint in her eyes that somehow eased the tension that had torn the confession from him.

"You deserve…"

He floundered, not knowing where to begin to list all the perfect, wonderful things she deserved. And while he was many things, perfect and wonderful were nowhere on the list.

"To have what I want? Thank you. Got it."

He hadn't expected the humor. Hadn't expected the pure, unadulterated joy that was shining in her face, that was washing over him as she smiled.

"Better," he muttered, finally finishing his previous sentence.

"Yes, much, thanks again." She didn't even try to hide that she was deliberately misunderstanding him.

"You know what I mean."

She sat up then. "Yes. I do. So isn't it a good thing that's not a decision you get to make?"

He stared at her, sitting there unabashedly naked, her nipples still taut from his mouth, and he was filled with a strange new emotion. Not the renewed lust he would have expected, although his body was certainly responding to the sight, but pride. Pride in her, at the strong, resilient woman she'd become, while losing none of her gentleness or tender heart.

"I need to go relieve Mom," she said as she rose, gathered up the clothes he'd tossed and began to dress. He watched avidly. She knew it, he knew she did, but she didn't seem to mind. After a moment he rose and reached for his own clothes, which had ended up strewn across the floor just as hers had. The memory of her urgency, of her hands frantically tugging at his shirt, the zipper of his jeans, nearly made him grab her and take her back to bed.

The thought made his hands shake slightly. He was out of control. He couldn't deny it any longer. The hell of it was, if being in control, if the thing he'd prided himself on for all these years, meant doing without what he'd found with her, he didn't want it back. But he had no choice.

"Dam?" She was there, beside him, and he hadn't even noticed her move. But she didn't touch him, as if she somehow knew he couldn't bear it at this moment.

"Can't risk this," he whispered.

She studied him silently. "You're not talking about ruining my election chances," she said at last.

"Jess—"

"It's us you can't risk. Me. Getting close."

"Your sake," he said, the words grating even to his own ears they were so harsh.

Hers, by contrast, went very soft. "Is that how you've spent all this time? Keeping people at bay, because of some idea you'll…hurt them?"

"Never wanted them to know…to face…"

"The life you lived? My God, the fact that you survived is nothing short of a miracle."

"Didn't break me."

"No, he didn't. You were too strong."

He shook his head, not feeling strong at all at the moment.

"You were. I can't even begin to imagine the kind of strength it took to do what you did at fourteen. Which means you're too strong to let what he did to you turn you into the same kind of monster he is."

She turned and grabbed her shoes, a pair of slip-on mocs, and pulled them on. Then she headed for the stairs that led down to the second floor of the house she'd grown up in.

"I may be thirty years old, but I'm still my mom's little girl, especially right now. If you're still here when she gets back, the explaining is up to you."

He gave the room one last glance, taking in every detail, filing it away. Then he started after her, not because he was afraid to face Naomi Hill, but because he didn't want to cause her any more pain. And thinking that her daughter had gotten tangled up with somebody like him could do nothing else.

He'd barely noticed the house itself before. He had been inside a couple of times in the old life, back before he'd heard the talk about how wicked he was and had begun to stay away despite Jessa's assurances her parents didn't feel that way. He saw now it hadn't changed a lot. Only the upstairs, Jessa's domain, looked different, more up-to-date. He found himself comparing the floral-print sofa and the heavy, swagged draperies to the clean stripes and bold blocks of color Jessa had used.

Only then did he realize he'd studied her room so carefully because he wanted a place for her to be, in his mind, when he thought of her in the future.

And because he knew he'd never see it again.

Chapter 22

Jessa looked up as the bell above the door rang. A tall, lean man came in, and looked around with interest. He was dressed like a local, in jeans, a plaid shirt and well-worn cowboy boots, but she didn't know him. Nor had she heard of any newcomers in town, news that usually traveled as fast as if they had that high-speed Internet she longed for.

She called out to the stranger, "If you need help finding anything, I'm the one to ask."

"I'm lookin'," the man said in a slow, easy drawl, "for Jessa Hill."

"That would be me," she said with a smile.

It occurred to her after she'd spoken that perhaps she should have been more cautious, that perhaps the rare visit of a complete stranger was another Alden machination, but one look into this man's steady gray eyes made that impossible for her to believe.

The man studied her for a long, silent moment, and Jessa had the feeling, despite the laid-back demeanor presented by the drawl, she was being sized up by an expert.

Then he ran a hand through slightly shaggy dark brown hair—she got the impression he usually had to lift a cowboy hat first—and an odd sort of smile curved his mouth.

"Well, well," he murmured, as if many things had just become clear to him. And as if those things surprised him greatly.

"Why do I get the feeling you're not here for horse feed?"

The man chuckled. "Time was, I could have been." An odd sort of shadow flickered in his eyes. "Not sure I don't prefer that time."

She understood too well the longing for a time past; she was standing in the biggest reminder she had of what she missed so much. Then the man shook his head as if to shake off the feeling, and held out his hand.

"Nice to meet you, Jessa Hill. I'm Josh Redstone."

She smothered a gasp, was certain she was doing the traditional double take, but couldn't help herself. She hadn't recognized him. She'd seen many photographs of the man, but mostly formal, posed portraits in a suit and tie, or distant shots where all you could see was his lanky frame and confident posture. And the boots, always the cowboy boots. She'd once smiled at one of the formal portraits, guessing he probably had a shinier pair on with the suit. There was nothing about him that spoke of the boardroom, he could have as easily been the ramrod of some vast cattle empire a century and a half ago as the shepherd of the global enterprise he was now.

Standing here in the flesh, he seemed nothing at all like those stiff portraits. She doubted anyone expecting the head of a worldwide empire would recognize him like this. The tousled, untrimmed hair, the worn clothes, the unwavering steadiness of his gaze, none of those could come across in two dimensions, not the way they did in reality.

She shook off her shock, and belatedly took the proffered hand. There was no challenge in it, just a firm, even grip. Perhaps he just didn't think a woman worth the effort, she thought, then decided as quickly as the thought formed that he wasn't the type. Men like this weren't threatened by such things.

"It's an honor, sir," she said as he released her hand. She put all the respect she felt into her tone, saw it register.

"Thank you," he said.

"I guess I don't have to ask why you're here, even if it's the last thing I expected."

He lifted a brow at her. "I see he's told you about me."

"Yes. After the figurative removal of several teeth, yes."

He laughed, with the rueful undertone of someone who knew exactly what it felt like trying to get information out of St. John.

And much later than she should have—it had to be the shock of having the man himself standing here—she realized what his first words, and the fact that he'd come here to the store, meant.

"I didn't realize he'd told you about me," she said.

"He didn't say much, but that he spoke of you at all…well, he doesn't talk a lot," he finished with the brief flash of a grin, "but I'm guessing you know that."

"That I do," she said wryly.

"It didn't take much to figure it out. All the pieces fit."

She looked at him curiously. "You know…about his life here?"

"Yes. I didn't know Cedar was the place, but what happened, yes. I got him drunk enough one night, long ago, to tell me, at least enough to understand."

Her brow furrowed.

"Don't worry," he said, although she didn't speak. "It was the one and only time, and I needed to know what he was dealing with to know how to deal with him."

"I wasn't judging," she said quickly. "I was just trying to imagine him surrendering that much control." A sudden image of Dam, naked, locked in her arms and completely out of control, flashed through her mind. She felt herself flush, and knew it had to be showing like a neon sign on her fair-skinned cheeks.

"Well, well," Josh said again, only this time there was a tone of awed wonder beneath the drawl.

She hastily changed the subject. "Did he ask you here?"

Josh shook his head. "No. But when my Vice President of Operations asks for time off for the first time in over a decade, vanishes, then starts some interesting wheels rolling, and then tries to stop them, I get…curious."

Jessa knew she was gaping again, but again couldn't help it. *Vice President of Operations of Redstone Incorporated?*

"He said he was…basically a gofer."

Josh laughed. "He would." Then he studied her for a moment before saying solemnly, as if he'd decided she'd earned it, "He's my right hand. He has the entire scope of Redstone in his head. He's our go-to guy for any crisis, and has built the most incredible network I've ever seen or heard of. He's probably the one person who could seamlessly step in if anything happened to me." And then, softly, he added, "And he's forever been the most alone man I've ever known."

She didn't think her expression changed, despite the twist of pain that tightened her chest.

"I knew," Josh said, "that there had been one bright spot in those ugly days. One thing that helped him to go on. That in a way, gave him the courage to escape the hell he was living in." His voice went even softer. "I'm guessing that bright spot was you."

Jessa felt her eyes start to brim. This was the man who had saved Dam, who had given him the chance at a kind of life she never would have dared hope for him. She wanted to hug the man, and would have if she wasn't so intimidated by the very idea of him standing here in her little store.

"Jess!"

She heard his voice from the back of the store, heard the urgency in it, and in the quick footsteps.

"Need to—"

Dameron St. John broke off, staring in shock at the man standing before her.

"What the hell?" he said, his voice harsh.

"Good to see you, too, my friend."

"Damn."

Josh took no offense, clearly realizing "you" wasn't attached to the word.

"That's the downside of having friends," Josh said, his drawl a bit more exaggerated as he looked with undisguised amusement at the man he'd called his right hand. "They keep sticking their nose in your business, because they care. Whether you want them to or not."

Jessa had to smother a laugh. The ache in her chest eased at the teasing; he'd had a friend, and obviously a good one, all these years.

Then she remembered the urgency with which he'd come in, before the shock of seeing his boss standing there had brought him to a halt.

"What do we need to do?" she asked.

He shook his head, almost fiercely. "Tyler."

She stiffened, worry sharpening her tone. "Is he all right?"

"May not be."

"What happened?"

"Sheriff's car."

"At the Alden house? Now?"

He nodded. "His."

"His car's there? He's supposed to be in River Mill today."

"Not."

"Too much to hope Tyler's mother finally called, I suppose," she said with a grimace.

"Yes."

"Let's go."

Whether it was her lack of any hesitation, or her assumption that they would deal with this together, she didn't know, but her simple declaration earned her a smile that warmed her to her core.

"Tyler wouldn't be a boy about ten or twelve with a cast on his arm, would he?"

They both spun to face Josh. He was watching them so intently Jessa was amazed they could have, even so focused on Tyler, almost forgotten he was there. Something, Jessa was sure, that didn't happen to Josh Redstone often, no matter how unassuming he was. And now there was the slightest of smiles on his face, and Jessa had the strangest feeling it had nothing to do with the subject at hand. And wondered if it had anything to do with the fact that she had easily followed Dam's cryptic conversation.

"I only ask," Josh said, "because he's in your barn out back."

Jessa and St. John both stared at him.

"I saw him when I pulled in. He darted back inside when he saw me."

They were outside in moments, heading toward the barn at a run. She was aware Josh was following, but Tyler was the objective for both of them now.

Maui met them at the door.

"Where is he, boy?" Jessa said softly.

The big dog turned and led them back to the stack of hay bales in the far corner of the barn. And there, barely visible protruding from behind the shelter of the bales, was a small shoe. Maui disappeared past the shoe, and it moved, Jessa guessed as the boy reached out to his gentle guardian.

"You," Jessa whispered to Dam. "It should be you."

She sensed him almost shake his head, knew he didn't want to do this, didn't think he could. She reached out, put a hand on his arm. His eyes closed for a moment, and he put his own hand over hers, squeezing in silent acknowledgment of the support.

"You're the only one who can really understand where he is right now."

His eyes opened. He nodded. Took in a deep breath. And took those last few steps forward.

Jessa stepped back until she was next to Josh. She glanced up at him, saw that he was staring at his Vice President of Operations with no small amount of amazement as Dam crouched down a foot away from that shoe that seemed impossibly small to her.

"Hey, buddy," Dam said quietly.

Jessa heard a murmur, but it was too quiet to understand from here.

"How bad is it?" Dam asked. Then, after another quiet answer, "You sure?"

He listened again to the boy's words, and while Jessa was anxious to know if Tyler was all right, she knew as well that interrupting them now could destroy a delicate balance.

"I know, Ty," he said, using the nickname he'd shyly told her he liked, that first day. "He told you it was your fault. That he had to beat the evil out of you. That he was a patient man, but you, you're so bad even a saint couldn't deal with you. And he told you if anything bad ever happened to your mother, it would be because of you."

She heard a sob then, wrenching, heart-breaking. She shivered, wrapping her arms around herself, nearly shaking with the pain she felt for that helpless child—and the pride she felt in the man stripping his long-protected soul bare to help him.

And then Tyler had moved, scrambling forward, throwing himself at Dam, tears streaming down a face that sported some new swelling besides the old black eye. Dam grabbed the boy, held him, sinking down to sit on the floor. It was all Jessa could do to stay where she was.

She felt a sudden warmth, a steady arm coming around her shoulders to lend her strength. Josh said nothing, was simply there, as intent on the emotional scene before them as she was. And she realized that he had seen none of the progression of the past weeks, and that the shock of seeing this St. John, compared to the one who had left Redstone, must be tremendous.

"He has to do this," she said, barely whispering so that the two on the floor couldn't hear. "He needs to."

"I know," Josh said, just as quietly. "I just never thought he would."

"And then," Dam said to the boy he held, "he gave you some hope. Said things would get better when you were a little older, and you were of some use to him."

Tyler looked up at him through his tears, and slowly nodded. "He…" The boy hiccupped, swallowed, tried again. She could hear him now, but Jessa almost wished she couldn't. "He said when I was twelve I could…do what sons do for their fathers. But he's not my father!"

"No." Dam tightened his grip on the shaking child. And then, with a grim, ugly note in his voice he finished. "He's mine."

Chapter 23

St. John sat on the bale of hay, wondering with a detached puzzlement why he was having so much trouble thinking. Maui sat beside him, leaning his full weight on his knee, occasionally sighing when St. John remembered to scratch that delicious spot behind his right ear.

Jessa sat beside him, but with that uncanny perceptiveness she seemed to have she didn't touch him. And he was, despite the hunger for her that never left him, grateful for that. He didn't think he could bear her gentle, loving touch, not right now. Right now he needed to stoke the anger, the fury at the twisted, evil being that was his father. And he couldn't seem to find it.

He felt simply exhausted. As if reaching into the depths of the darkness inside him to help Tyler had somehow drained it away, leaving him a hollow shell with no energy, no strength, no fire.

"Josh?" he asked wearily.

"They're gone."

After a moment to process the answer, he gave a slight nod.

Unlike him, Josh had been able to gain, if not Tyler's trust then at least his cooperation, within a matter of minutes. Of course, the fact that the boy had actually heard of him—the news of Redstone's interest in Riverside Paper had apparently been a loud topic in the Alden house—and knew his stepfather was furious about it, likely put Josh on his good side. And the promise of actually getting to set foot on Josh's plane was irresistible.

With Tyler safely out of the line of fire, St. John knew it was time. It was time to put an end to all of this. But he couldn't seem to find the energy to even move.

Maui's trumpeting bark penetrated the fog in his mind. The dog leaped to his feet. His demeanor was something St. John had never seen from the sweet-natured animal, hackles up and tail still and held straight out behind him; this was not Josh coming back. The dog bolted for the door of the barn, head down, ears back.

Jessa was on her feet and following in an instant, her focus on her beloved dog. Trying to shake off this unsettling lethargy, St. John got to his feet; whatever had the dog riled up, he wasn't about to let Jessa face it on her own, no matter what he was feeling like.

Nearly simultaneously he heard three things; Maui's yelp of pain, Jessa's cry of protest, and a man's voice.

His father's voice.

"Get that damned mutt away from me! I've called the sheriff, he's on his way over here. You're going to finally get yours, you arrogant bitch. What have you done with the boy?"

He exploded into a run and was at the barn door in two seconds. Maui was crouched at Jessa's feet, growling fiercely, only her slender hand on his collar holding him back. And Albert Alden was too damn close to her, looming over her as she put herself between him and the angry dog.

"Where is my son? I know he's here, one of my idiot

neighbors finally got around to telling me you've been showing up at my house with this mangy dog."

"And only a coward would take his problem with me out on a dog," Jessa snapped, facing him down with a steadfast glare. "Or a child."

Alden flushed, cocked his arm back as if to strike, but hesitated as St. John skidded to a halt and firmly pulled Jessa behind him.

"One finger on her or that dog, you're dead where you stand."

In that moment St. John knew he meant it, more than he ever had in his life. And when his father turned to face him, puzzlement on his face, he realized with a sudden rush that Jessa's words had been true. He'd called himself a coward for hiding, setting himself apart from the world, when in truth it was this man who was the coward. And he always had been.

"Who the hell are you? And what business is it of yours?"

"What you've done is every decent person's business," Jessa said, and as he flicked a quick glance at her, St. John thought she'd never been more beautiful than she was in that moment, fierce, fearless and facing down his demon for him.

His father didn't even look at her, he was staring at St. John. "I've seen you around town. You're helping her, aren't you?" Realization dawned on his flushed face. "That explains it. I knew she was too stupid to have done this on her own. You're some kind of consultant or something, aren't you?"

St. John inwardly gathered himself, knowing the battle he'd postponed for more than half his life was at hand. He focused on the man before him, feeling the weight of the last twenty years, knowing that one way or another that weight was about to be relieved.

"You're good, I'll give you that," Alden said, his tone changing completely, turning, incredibly, coaxing, persuasive.

"I can pay you more, you know. Better to work for the winner."

"Save your money. You'll need a lawyer."

Alden frowned. "Look, I don't know what this stupid fool has told you, but it's not true. She's just desperate because she knows she's going to lose, so she's trying to smear me."

St. John went very still. "Jess," he said quietly. His gaze never left the face of the man who had once haunted his nightmares. His father was still studying him, but not with the expression of someone who thought he recognized him but couldn't place him. It was more of a calculating look, as if he were trying to put him in a prelabeled slot that would tell him how to deal with him. "Take Maui. Go home."

"I'm not leaving you here with him!" she exclaimed.

"Afraid I'll kill him? Might."

He took a small amount of pleasure in the fact that Alden straightened suddenly, and backed up a half step. And a bit more pleasure in the fact that for a moment fear showed in his eyes, beneath the puzzlement.

Yes, be afraid, he thought as he let the rage he'd kept in check for so long lose a notch.

"Don't you dare threaten me! You know who I am."

"Precisely."

"Then you know I'm an important man, that I could…"

Alden's voice trailed away as St. John silently stared at him. He didn't have Draven's stare-down ability, but he'd seen how it worked on some scary enemies, and Albert Alden was a much lesser, slimier creature.

It was only to him that the man was the archetype of evil.

Only to him…and Jessa. For his sake.

The thought warmed him. And for the first time in his life he realized that there was something more important than this man. He may have bent him, twisted him, shaped him, but Jessa had brought him back to life in a way he'd never imagined.

He looked at her then, because he had to. She was watching him, her eyes full of anguish and worry. For him. Some new, fierce emotion ripped through him, something so big he knew he couldn't deal with it now.

And he knew he couldn't deal with her witnessing this.

"Jess. Go. Please."

He was almost surprised when, after a moment's contemplation, of studying his face, of looking as if that agile mind of hers was racing, she nodded. She whispered to Maui and led the dog back toward the store. Alden watched her go, looking as if he wanted to go after her. Typical, he thought, to want to go after the prey he would consider weaker, and probably only leery because of the dog.

She's not one of the frightened, cowering women you prefer, St. John thought, knowing that Jessa would fight him with every weapon she had, including that quick mind and a warrior's heart.

And that knowledge renewed a steely resolve to never, ever let that happen.

Apparently deciding against his urges for once, Alden shifted his gaze back to St. John.

"What has she done with that little brat of mine?"

The rage, so deeply buried, uncoiled a bit more. "He's not yours."

"I've legally adopted him, despite his problems. Everyone knows how difficult it's been. He's such a problem." Even now, St. John thought, he couldn't stop the campaign rhetoric. It was automatic, as was the long-suffering sigh as he added. "But I still treat him like he's my own."

"That," St. John said, his voice ice, "I believe."

Something in that voice got to Alden. He stared, as if he'd finally understood there was something much more going on here.

Finally, sounding shaken, he whispered, "Who are you?"

It was time, St. John knew. Time to end it all. Delaying,

hesitating, gave the man power. With conscious intention, he let the ferocious beast within him loose.

"Grooming Tyler, are you?" he said with a calm precision that made the words even more intense. "That's why you're so upset he's gone."

"Of course I'm upset." Alden said it imperiously, but St. John could almost smell the uncertainty beneath the words; he was still wondering what he was up against, and with that shrewd cunning he'd always had, he knew it wasn't just some generic political consultant.

"He's almost the right age, isn't he? And you've almost gotten him beaten down enough, when you make your move he'll be too frightened to resist. He'll let you do it, let you commit your twisted, ugly, perverted sins, because you've convinced him he has no other choice. But inside he'll start wondering, if maybe death wouldn't be better, better than this."

It was more than he'd said in one breath in years. But once he'd begun, once the walls had been breached and the beast freed, it had come easier, faster.

"I don't have the slightest idea what you're talking about," Alden said, diving back into an explanation that came so smoothly St. John knew he'd used it many times before. "The boy needs discipline, yes, but boys do. They need a strong hand."

Memories of that "strong hand" churned. St. John quashed them. It was harder, here in the presence of evil, but even they were no match for the beast.

"You'll convince him that finally he can do something right, that this is the way to please you, to submit to your twisted, perverted needs."

"How dare you! I don't have to stand here and listen to this garbage."

He began to turn as if to go, his concern for his stepson apparently forgotten. St. John's voice lowered to a whisper that conveyed every bit of the deadly rage he was feeling. And he delivered the words that he knew Alden would recognize.

"You'll tell him it's a special thing, a rite of passage. That this is what sons do for their fathers."

Alden stopped dead. Stared at him. No denial broke through his shocked bafflement. No anger at an unjust accusation, no righteous indignation. Not even another threat.

"Who *are* you?" This time it was a hoarse, choked whisper.

St. John knew he was closing in now. On some level he was aware of movement off to one side, but didn't look that way or veer from his course. He knew who was there, could almost feel her presence, he didn't have to look.

"I'm hurt," he said with feigned chagrin. "You don't even recognize me."

Alden looked him up and down, as if he were seeing him for the first time. Denial was clear on his face, and calculation, as he tried to figure out how much this stranger knew and how he knew it.

"Don't bother. I don't look like him anymore. More important, I don't think like him."

"Like…who?"

"I've got to hand it to you. Not many could take the onus of two suicides and still build a power base."

"Two suicides? My son drowned in a horrible storm, everyone knows that."

"Except those who knew—or suspected—the truth. And your son, of course. Which did you miss most, your plaything, or the money he took out of the cash box? Or maybe the fancy money clip you prized so much?"

"Who are you?" Alden nearly screamed it this time. And St. John saw, deep in the furtive, too-glassy eyes, the dawning of knowledge he'd been waiting for.

"You know who I am. Torturing me was once the prime focus of your warped, disgusting life."

"That's impossible. He's dead!"

"Ever hear the legend of the phoenix?"

Alden shook his head, but his face was pasty white. "You can't be. You look nothing like him."

"Modern surgery's a wonderful thing. They fixed that jawbone you broke so badly I couldn't eat for a month. Took that dent out of that cheekbone you shattered. And while they were at it, they erased the rest of the face you used to use as a punching bag."

"No. No," Alden said, backing up a step.

"I kept this one, though," St. John said, touching the remaining scar. "It's the one I got that night at the river. The one you didn't give me. It's my badge, my reminder to never let anyone own me again."

St. John saw it hit, saw the denial die away as his father confronted the fact of who was actually before him. And then, belatedly, what that fact meant.

"Yes," he said softly. "I'm the man who's going to bring down your house of cards. The man who's going to end it all. Take it all away from you. Everything you crave—including Tyler—is gone or going. And you can't do a thing to stop it."

Alden shook his head, but there was a touch of panic in the motion.

"And if you're thinking you'll slip away, maybe escape to the Caymans and live on your pile of cash you've been squirreling away, think again. It's gone, too."

Alden's eyes went wider, and St. John knew he'd thought of it, thought of his bolt hole, and imagined his fear as the last option was erased.

"And it's all going to come out. Everything you've done, to Jessa, to Tyler, to my mother...to me. All of it."

"It's all lies!" The panic had made it's way to his voice. "No one will believe you. No one will even listen to you."

"Think not? Want to know where Tyler really is?"

"No one will believe him, either."

"Counted on that, didn't you? Just like you did with me. But Tyler's got help now."

"If you mean that little bitch—"

St. John unleashed the blow before he'd even realized he was doing it. He felt the smash of pain in his knuckles in the instant before his father hit the ground.

And then Jessa was beside him. "Before you actually kill him," she said, as if she were discussing nothing more serious than her supply of bird seed, "you should know half the town's here."

So that was what he'd sensed. Jessa had brought the cavalry. Or at least, witnesses.

"I won't. He's not worth it."

Jessa took his hand, squeezed it. "No, he's not. And what he'll be facing will be worse than death, to him."

Alden was gingerly getting up when St. John realized she'd meant it, that there were at least twenty people standing in the yard between the back of the store and the barn, staring at him in shock, what they'd heard reflected in their expressions of horror and disgust.

"He didn't mean I'm Tyler's help," she said, eyeing Alden much as she would have a worm-infested sack of feed. St. John was oddly starting to enjoy this at last, now that Jessa was here. "If you're really wondering where Tyler is—which I doubt, the only thing you're worried about now is yourself— he's with someone *everyone* will believe."

"Mr. Alden?" The voice that came from behind him spun Alden around. A man in a sheriff's uniform was closing in, his jaw set as if he didn't care for the task at hand. A second deputy was behind him. "You'll need to come with me, sir. Some very serious allegations have been made."

"I'm not going anywhere with you!" He gestured at St. John and Jessa. "I don't know what they've told you, but it's all a pack of lies!"

The deputy frowned. "Actually, the charges were made by an outside source. A very credible one."

"What?" Alden said blankly. "Who?"

"Joshua Redstone."

St. John saw Alden's expression change at the sound of the famous name. And heard a murmur ripple through the gathered watchers.

"What the hell does he have to do with anything?" Alden demanded.

"My boss," St. John said simply.

"And," Jessa added quietly, "one of his oldest, closest friends. You," she added, her tone suddenly one of deep relish, "are going down."

Alden swore, backed up a step. The deputy took his arm. When he tried to jerk away, the second deputy stepped up quickly and took the other.

"Hard and ugly," St. John added, his voice, in contrast to the words, almost sunny.

"You son of a bitch!" He was staring wild-eyed at the man who had been his son. "I was glad to be rid of you. You were getting too old for me anyway."

The gathered townspeople gasped in unison. Alden seemed startled, as if he'd forgotten there were witnesses, and so many of them. He looked at them, saw what was there, in their shocked—and believing—expressions. The Redstone name had tilted the balance completely, and Alden knew it.

"Damn you!" he yelled. "Damn you to hell!"

"Already did your best on that," St. John said.

"And failed," Jessa said. "He's so much stronger than you. He always was."

"You," Alden spat out. "I always knew there was something between you two. I knew you were—"

"You knew nothing about me," St. John cut him off, his tone so calm now it was even more ominous than when the rage had been loosed. "Just like you know nothing about Tyler. And now you never will."

Alden tried futilely to pull free, but the deputies, who looked convinced now themselves, only tightened their grip.

And one, belatedly seeing the light, took a pair of handcuffs from his belt and slapped them around Alden's wrists, the distinctive ratcheting sound seemingly the final punctuation mark. Albert Alden drained like a punctured abscess. Spittle gleamed on his chin as he stared at the son he hadn't seen in twenty years.

"Tyler was a poor substitute," he said.

St. John went rigid.

"You'll never forget," Alden said, for the first time the pure evil of his soul showing in his eyes. His voice was bloodcurdlingly gentle as he added, "And neither will I. Nothing feels as good as your own flesh and blood."

Jessa's grip tightened on his hand, and in that moment her touch was the only thing that kept him anchored, the only thing that kept him from slaughtering this monster where he stood.

Chapter 24

"Tyler will be fine," Josh assured her. "Redstone will see to that."

Jessa nodded; she'd only known Josh Redstone a few hours, but she already knew he meant what he said and would get it done.

"I've got good people with the Westin Foundation who have a lot of experience dealing with traumatized kids."

Jessa nodded again. "I wish something like that had been around for him," she said quietly.

She didn't have to explain who she meant—she knew Josh knew all too well. "It's a wonder he functions as incredibly well as he does," Josh said. "And I'm thinking we may need to expand the foundation, a program to deal with the aftermath of things like this."

Then, looking at her steadily, he went on. "You know he's already at the plane."

"He's going to run, isn't he?"

Josh nodded. "For now. And probably, occasionally, forever. Can you deal with that?"

"I know he'll never be the same as a man who had a normal childhood. But I also know how strong he is, what it took for him to get to where he is from where he started."

"Don't give up on him, Jessa."

"I won't. Ever. He won't let it rule him. Not once he gets through all this, and the pain of confronting it all when he'd thought he left it behind forever."

Josh smiled at her, a warm, welcoming sort of smile.

"That you know tells me you are indeed what I'd hoped. You'll be his final salvation, Jessa."

She shook her head. "I'm just me. I can't save him. I couldn't before, either. But he can save himself. He's that strong."

"Yes, he is. Not many could see that, with his leaving you like this. But it's there, Jessa. He's running from possibilities he's afraid to believe in, because he once had to run from a reality too ugly to be borne."

"I know."

"Give it some time. Then call me. Or I'll call you when he's in a better place than he is right now."

The idea of calling the great Josh Redstone made her smile. "Sure. I'll just pick up the phone and demand to talk to one of the most important men in the world."

"I'm just me." Josh repeated her words with obvious full intent. "And I'll always take a call from you."

Jessa looked into his smoky-gray eyes, seeing what so many others had seen. "I understand now why Redstone is what it is. Because you are what you are."

"Redstone is its people. Always has been." He reached out and put a warm, gentle hand on her shoulder as he looked at her intently. "Always will be."

When he was gone, she wondered if there had been some extra meaning, directed at her, in those last words.

St. John shivered as he shook off the icy water, but he made himself focus on every aspect of his being. The cold from the lake, the further chill of the slight breeze on his wet body, the contrasting warmth of the sun that managed to penetrate through the canopy of the trees, the sensation of being clean again, physically at least, and the rough feel of his beard as he rubbed a hand over the jaw he hadn't shaved in nearly a week.

He knew if he stepped just a few yards to his right, he would be in a patch of full sun, and the shivering would ease. He pondered for a moment if he should allow himself that. He wasn't certain. Wasn't certain he had rebuilt the cage strongly enough to keep the old memories at bay.

He hadn't expected that vanquishing the fiend who had contributed half his DNA would erase it all. Nothing could. So he hadn't even hung around to follow the sensational stories of his spectacular downfall. He knew there would likely be a day in court—he couldn't picture the man who had haunted him going down that easily—when he would have to publicly tell the story.

He dreaded that day, but he could hardly leave Tyler to carry that load alone. And he was alone; his mother, incredibly, had sided with her bread and butter, and was vowing to stand beside her husband to the end. The boy was with a foster family vetted by the Westin Foundation, and St. John knew from his own experience that the relief would be nothing short of life-altering.

Life-altering.

And there it was again. The realization that his time in Cedar, his time with Jessa, had been just that. Life-altering.

And yet he'd left her. Without a word of explanation why. And no contact in the month since. She'd probably given up on him, and would eventually find some sane, normal man who could give her the kind of life she deserved—decent, sane and happy.

The thought made his gut twist worse than remembering his father's abuse had.

He had to get a grip, he told himself. It's what he was here for. Josh had sent him to this remote cabin in the woods of

Washington State, a place Josh himself went to often, for exactly that quality; the setting and the opportunity not to see another soul for weeks on end. The only sign of civilization he'd seen or heard in the last month was the occasional distant sound of a vehicle on the rural gravel road, and as he'd started his walk to the lake this morning, the sound of the Forest Service helicopter that went over now and then.

"You deserve time and space to regroup," Josh had said. "It's a good place for that." And then, with that piercing insight that had helped him build Redstone into the amazing thing it was, he'd added, "But don't kid yourself, Dam. Don't keep running from the one thing that might actually balance out what was done to you."

Jess....

He made no sound, but his mind screamed it, the name he couldn't bear to say. He shivered again, but this time it wasn't so much from the cold. Abruptly he decided he was dry enough, and besides, he'd welcome the battle of trying to drag clothes over damp skin.

He paused in the act of dressing when a strange tickle crept up his spine to the back of his neck. His head came up sharply. While these woods were relatively safe, the biggest predator generally seen being the ubiquitous coyote, the occasional bear wasn't unheard of.

He glanced around, looking for anything big enough to be threatening.

What he found was petite, blond and a bigger threat than any creature who made its home in these woods.

"Jess...."

It escaped him this time, that name he'd never expected to speak again.

For a moment he thought he might be hallucinating, some aftereffect of the shockingly cold water, or the fact that he'd been isolated here for so long. And then she stepped out of the shadows into that patch of sunlight. It turned her tousled crop of hair impossibly golden, she looked like some delicate forest elf caught for a moment in the human realm. But he knew she was real. His fingers curled with the knowledge, the memory of that slender body, of that sleek, satin skin, of the fiery, slick heat of her in those moments when he'd found a joy he'd never thought to know.

His body roused to the memory, so swiftly that for a moment he couldn't catch his breath, and his half-zipped jeans threatened to retreat. He walked toward her, unable to stop himself. But the moment he stepped into the sunlight, he stopped, as unable to go on as he'd been unable to stop.

"What are you doing here?"

"Looking for—and at—you," she said, almost teasingly.

Remembering what he'd just been doing, standing here naked and wet, lost in his ridiculous ponderings, he couldn't help asking, "How long…?"

"Long enough," she said with a look in her eyes that echoed the hunger he was sure was glowing in his own. "Did I ever tell you how beautiful you are?"

She said it with such simple wonder that he knew she believed it, even if he couldn't even begin to. Still a little stunned at her sudden, unexpected presence, and realizing he was far from regrouped if just her appearance could rattle him like this, he groped for a diversion.

"How did you…?"

He didn't finish this question, either, as the obvious answer dawned on him. It hadn't been a Forest Service helicopter at all.

"Tess is remarkable," Jess said, as casually as if they were discussing what trees grew here. "I never would have thought you could land a helicopter in that tiny clearing, but she did it without turning a hair."

"Josh," he muttered.

"Yes. Sweet of him to loan me his personal pilot, wasn't it?"

"Interfering."

"Depends on your point of view, I guess," she said, not rising to the bait.

"Go."

"No."

"Your own sake."

"The last person I voluntarily took that kind of order from was my father. He wouldn't want me to take it now." Unexpectedly, she grinned. "You know, I've kind of missed your shorthand. It makes for…exhilarating conversation."

He was digging too deep to really appreciate the humor. "Not safe."

"I've never been safer."

"Not worth it."

"With most, perhaps. But with you there's a difference, Dam. Most people build walls to keep people out. Yours are built to keep the part of you you're afraid is too damaged away from people. To keep them safe, not yourself. Don't you see that's…noble?"

He couldn't even answer that assessment, it seemed so ridiculous. Noble? Hardly.

He was shivering again, although his clothes had absorbed the last of the water, and he wasn't that chilled anymore, standing here in the sun. With her.

"That's a perfectly acceptable way of dealing with it, you know. Walling it off, I mean."

"Not whole."

"Sure you are," she said briskly.

How, he wondered, had she known that gentleness, softness, would cripple him just now?

She went on in the same tone. "There's just a part of you that you need to guard more than most. But it's like having a dent in a car that runs perfectly, or a drafty spot in a house you love, that you only notice when the wind blows a certain way. Do you junk the car, tear down the house?"

He shook his head, not in negation but to try and clear it, to try and make sense of the chaotic thoughts that were careening around in his head.

"It was him," he murmured, barely aware of speaking it aloud.

"I know you know it was all his fault, not yours, that's not news," Jessa said. "So what is it that was him?"

"My drive. Ambition. All him. He really did make me what I am. Hating him did. Without it, I'm…"

His voice trailed away. *Without it,* he thought, *I'm nothing. Hating him made me what I am. And now I feel…nothing.*

"Without it," Jessa said, "you're still you. Don't you see, Dam? You took what he did to you, what he forced you to learn just to survive, and you used it, turned it back on him. He tried to convince you you were useless, stupid, bad and God knows what else. And you didn't just prove him wrong, you proved *him* useless, stupid and bad. And pure evil into the bargain."

Again he was shivering, and he couldn't seem to stop. Jessa never let up. She wouldn't, he thought almost numbly. There was no quit, no give up in her.

"Think about it," she urged. "You surpassed him long ago. You're so far above his treasured 'status' he'll choke on it. Rub it in. Make him look as small as he is in comparison. I mean, what's a small-town country lawyer next to the Vice President of Operations for Redstone Incorporated?"

Somehow he had never thought of it like that.

"He doesn't deserve your hate, Dam. Not that he isn't evil, he just doesn't deserve one more ounce of your energy." She took a deep breath before adding, "But we do."

He shook his head again, in pain this time.

"You deserve—"

"I think I told you once that's a decision you don't get to make."

"Jess—"

"The only decision you have to make is if you're going to let him win, after all."

She was, in her way, as merciless as he'd ever thought of being. And as determined. He could feel it, coming off her in waves. She was her own kind of warrior, and she would leave this battlefield with victory, or not at all.

"If you let what he did to you run your life," she said fiercely, "for the rest of your life, then he wins, Dam. Then that evil monster has done what he wanted all along. He's broken you."

His shivers turned to a violent shudder. A sudden weakness sent him to his knees. And in an instant Jessa was there, on her own knees beside him, holding him.

"Don't let him," she said, her voice taut. "Don't let him win, please."

He leaned into her soft warmth, needing her gentleness now as he couldn't have taken it before, and beyond wondering how she'd sensed the change.

He couldn't speak, and she thankfully didn't press him, just held him, tightly, and he had the odd sensation that she was literally holding him together while the emotions ripping at him were trying to tear him apart. Destroy him.

Because he realized now, probably had the instant he'd seen her step into that shaft of golden sunlight, that he could no longer exist the way he'd been for the last twenty years. So his choice was even more basic than Jessa realized…he either did as she asked, or he died. It was that simple.

Her arm tightened around him, fiercely, almost as if she'd followed his thoughts, as if she knew what choice he'd arrived at.

"I want you to think of something," she said softly. "I want you to think of your father, sitting in that cell he's in, finally where he belongs, knowing he's been beaten at last. And then think of him smiling that evil, vicious, depraved smile when he learns that he's won after all, that he's destroyed you."

He shuddered again, violently, because the image she painted was too clear, the memory of that very smile too vivid. He would smile like that, with twisted, perverted pleasure, if he heard that the son he'd abused had, even now, given up the battle.

And there, in that forest, in the dappled sunlight that sparkled off a glassy lake, he knew he didn't want to die. She was right. He knew she was right. If he let this rule him, the bastard won. And he might as well end it right here and now rather than let this cripple him.

Let it cripple them.

He just doesn't deserve one more ounce of your energy. But we do.

He shuddered once more. Was he a fool, daring to want more than the walled-off life he'd allowed himself? And a bigger fool for thinking that maybe, just maybe, the Redstone magic that had brought so many others together might actually apply to him?

It wasn't that he didn't know what he wanted—he did. What he wanted was right here, holding him, giving him a kind of support he'd never had—except from the child she'd been. He wanted everything she could give him, her love, her warmth, her tenderness, her courage....

And he realized that was what he lacked. Her courage. The courage to refuse to give a twisted, perverted man power over him. The courage to truly leave behind the past. Or at the least, to wall it up securely enough that it withered and died from lack of attention and feeding.

It was a long time later that Jessa spoke. "I take it back."

For an instant his gut knotted in the old way as he wondered automatically if she'd finally seen the light and changed her mind, decided to walk away from a man too damaged for her sunny goodness. But a newfound knowledge and faith quashed the thought before he spoke; this was Jessa, steadfast, unwavering. She wouldn't. She just wouldn't. And her next words proved him right.

"There's another decision you have to make."

"What?" He was surprised at how steady his voice was.

"I know I'm all tied up in your mind with the bad times. Will I always remind you? Can you let go of that?"

"You're...the only thing I want to keep. From then."

"You don't get over the kind of things that happened to you. I know that. You can only figure out how to live with them, around them. It's pretty obvious you've learned that. And that Redstone's become the family you should have had, but didn't. You trust them. I know what a miracle that alone is."

So did he. He hadn't really realized it before he'd gone back to Cedar, but he knew it now.

She went on, gently but relentlessly, that warrior closing in.

"And I know you'll need time, now and then, to come to someplace like this, rebuild those walls. And I'm okay with that."

He felt a new, fiercer kind of tightness that seemed to encompass his entire body as her gentle words and her uncanny understanding washed over him. He hadn't needed this before, this escape to rebuild the walls, because he'd never been close enough to anyone that it mattered.

It mattered now.

"That is," she went on, "I'm okay with it as long as we get an equal amount of time away. Josh says you work too hard. That you never sleep."

"Sleep...isn't always good."

"Nightmares? I think I know how to fix that," she said, with a look that sent his pulse racing. "So what you have to decide is...if you want me. If you want us."

He sucked in a breath. Steadied himself. And looked up to meet her eyes. Clear, honest, beautiful eyes. Eyes in which he could see the future, the chance at things he never even dared to wish for, if only he could find the nerve to reach for it. And somehow, what he saw there gave him that nerve.

"More," he said slowly, "than I've ever wanted anything. *Anything.*"

He saw in her face, in her eyes, that she understood the import of his words. That he wanted the precious "us" she'd spoken of more than he'd even wanted to destroy the man who had nearly destroyed him.

"Kids. Can't," he said, knowing she'd understand.

"After the way you were with Tyler? I wouldn't worry at all. We could adopt. But if you want, we'll raise dogs instead. Borrow kids. I understand there's a few of them available at Redstone."

"Work."

"I know. You have to be there. That may take me some time, until Mom's in a little better shape. But I've always wanted to see California."

"Election."

"I withdrew." She grinned, startling him. "The town council appointed a temporary mayor, in light of circumstances."

"Who?"

"Uncle Larry."

He blinked. Nearly smiled at the very thought.

"I never really wanted it anyway," she said.

"That's who should hold office."

"Those who don't really want the power? I agree. Larry sees it as a temporary but necessary nuisance in his life. I think that's the right attitude."

She reached up then, her gentle fingers tracing the scar. He shuddered under her touch, unable to hide the reaction, and deep down, not wanting to.

"No one will ever own you again, Dam."

He shook his head. "Wrong."

"What?"

He knew what he was about to admit, knew it down to his bones. And knew it had to be. Because it had always been.

"You do. Want you to."

The smile that curved her mouth then made him think of a long, unbroken string of mornings, waking to that smile. And then, in a voice full of so much emotion it sounded nearly a shaky as he felt, she said, "I love you, Dameron St. John. Just as I loved Adam Alden. And I always will."

He swallowed tightly. "I know. And it makes me feel like… for the first time in my life…I… God, Jess, is this love? Is this what it feels like? Too big to hold, so huge you think you're going to explode into pieces?"

"That," she said, "is exactly what it feels like."

"Then…I…"

He couldn't quite get the words he'd never said out. But it didn't seem to matter to Jessa. She simply looked at him, that smile widening.

"I know," she said softly, in answer to what he hadn't said. And much later, in the dappled sunlight that played across two sleek, naked bodies locked together, he found the words.

It was in the quiet aftermath that he reached over to his discarded jeans and dug into the pocket. He found what he was looking for, tugged it out. And held it up for her to see.

When Jessa focused on the clay dog dangling from the keychain she'd given him so long ago, her beautiful, changeable eyes widened. And the smile she gave him then held all he needed to know of the future.

Epilogue

"This place is buzzing like a power saw convention," John Draven said as he walked into his boss's office. "Never seen anything like it. Is it for real?"

Josh sat behind his desk, but he was staring out the windows to the west, toward the ocean. The view was the only thing in this surprisingly—for a billionaire—spare office that spoke of what this man had achieved in a relatively short time. But Josh was all about function, not show, and Draven knew he always had been.

For a long moment Josh said nothing, and Draven could only imagine what was going through his mind.

"So it seems," Josh finally answered, but he still didn't turn to look at his Chief of Security.

"You told me once," Draven said softly, "that if you heard St. John was getting married, then you'd know the world was coming to an end."

"And it may well be," Josh said under his breath, so quietly Draven knew it would be better if he pretended not to have heard it. And then Josh seemed to shake it off, and at last turned to look at him.

"It's right?" Draven asked.

"Very," Josh said. "She's probably the only woman in the world who could deal with him, with what he has to live with. And God knows he's earned what he's found. Paid for it in the hardest way." Humor flickered in Josh's eyes. "And the fact that he's so surprised and stunned about it is the icing on the cake."

Draven couldn't help smiling at the very idea of St. John in either of those states. "Who is she?" Draven asked.

"From what he told me, she's the only reason he was still alive for us to meet, all those years ago."

Draven sat down on the scarred leather couch that Josh had had for years, since the early days in the hangar. It sat facing the other way, toward the Redstone Headquarters central courtyard, with its cool green garden and peaceful pond and waterfall. Josh expected the most out of his people, but he also gave them the most, and that garden was a favorite spot of most who worked here in the building.

"Then we owe her," Draven said.

"Yes."

"You know, don't you? What happened to him? What made him...who he is?"

"Yes. For the most part. I doubt anyone knows the whole ugly truth." As if in counterpoint to the unpleasant acknowledgment, a smile curved Josh's mouth. "Except, I'm guessing, Jessa Hill."

"Can't wait to meet her."

"You'll like her. She's...just what you'd hope."

What he hoped, Draven thought, now that the unthinkable had happened and the Redstone magic had transformed not just his own hardened heart, but even the legendary St. John's, was for the one thing that would cause even more buzz. The one thing that would delight all of Redstone, a bit of the happiness they'd found for the man they owed it all to.

Once, before his own life had changed so incredibly for the better, he would have never thought such a thing. Now he, and most of Redstone he guessed, wished for nothing less than the biggest dose of Redstone magic to happen to their beloved boss.

"It could happen," his own sweet Grace had said this morning when she'd heard the impossible news about St. John. "If it could happen for him, it could happen for Josh."

"Like it happened for us," he'd said.

"Yes. And still does," she'd purred, and proceeded to make him late getting here.

"There must be," Josh said musingly, "something in the Redstone water."

Draven pulled himself out of the hot, sweet memory of this morning and back to the present. "More like something in the Redstone people. When you bring together the best, people who think in the Redstone way, it's going to happen."

When he left a few minutes later, Josh was back to staring out the window.

And battle-hardened, intimidating, ruthless John Draven was aching inside for the man who had given so much and taken so little.

It could happen....

"Then let it be soon," he muttered to himself.

And he knew that there wasn't a single person in this building who wouldn't echo his sentiments.

But sitting around hoping wasn't the Redstone way. And it certainly wasn't his. Action was. He just wasn't sure what action to take. But he'd figure it out.

He was Redstone, after all.

*Rancher Ramsey Westmoreland's temporary cook
is way too attractive for his liking.
Little does he know Chloe Burton came to his ranch
with another agenda entirely....*

That man across the street had to be, without a doubt, the most handsome man she'd ever seen.

Chloe Burton's pulse beat rhythmically as he stopped to talk to another man in front of a feed store. He was tall, dark and every inch of sexy—from his Stetson to the well-worn leather boots on his feet. And from the way his jeans and Western shirt fit his broad muscular shoulders, it was quite obvious he had everything it took to separate the men from the boys. The combination was enough to corrupt any woman's mind and had her weakening even from a distance. Her body felt flushed. It was hot. Unsettled.

Over the past year the only male who had gotten her time and attention had been the e-mail. That was simply pathetic, especially since now she was practically drooling simply at the sight of a man. Even his stance—both hands in his jeans pockets, legs braced apart, was a pose she would carry to her dreams.

And he was smiling, evidently enjoying the conversation being exchanged. He had dimples, incredibly sexy dimples in not one but both cheeks.

"What are you staring at, Clo?"

Chloe nearly jumped. She'd forgotten she had a lunch date. She glanced over the table at her best friend from college, Lucia Conyers.

"Take a look at that man across the street in the blue shirt, Lucia. Will he not be perfect for Denver's first issue of *Simply Irresistible* or what?" Chloe asked with so much excitement she almost couldn't stand it.

She was the owner of *Simply Irresistible*, a magazine for today's up-and-coming woman. Their once-a-year Irresistible

Man cover, which highlighted a man the magazine felt deserved the honor, had increased sales enough for Chloe to open a Denver office.

When Lucia didn't say anything but kept staring, Chloe's smile widened. "Well?"

Lucia glanced across the booth at her. "Since you asked, I'll tell you what I see. One of the Westmorelands—Ramsey Westmoreland. And yes, he'd be perfect for the cover, but he won't do it."

Chloe raised a brow. "He'd get paid for his services, of course."

Lucia laughed and shook her head. "Getting paid won't be the issue, Clo—Ramsey is one of the wealthiest sheep ranchers in this part of Colorado. But everyone knows what a private person he is. Trust me—he won't do it."

Chloe couldn't help but smile. The man was the epitome of what she was looking for in a magazine cover and she was determined that whatever it took, he would be it.

"Umm, I don't like that look on your face, Chloe. I've seen it before and know exactly what it means."

She watched as Ramsey Westmoreland entered the store with a swagger that made her almost breathless. She *would* be seeing him again.

Look for Silhouette Desire's
HOT WESTMORELAND NIGHTS by Brenda Jackson,
available March 9 wherever books are sold.

Copyright © 2010 by Brenda Streater Jackson

ROMANTIC

SUSPENSE

Sparked by Danger, Fueled by Passion.

Introducing a brand-new miniseries
Lawmen of Black Rock

Peyton Wilkerson's life shatters when her
four-month-old daughter, Lilly, vanishes.
But handsome sheriff Tom Grayson is
determined to put the pieces together and
reunite her with her baby. Will Tom be able
to protect Peyton and Lilly while fighting
his own growing feelings?

Find out in
His Case, Her Baby
by
CARLA CASSIDY

Available in March wherever books are sold

Visit Silhouette Books at www.eHarlequin.com

SRS27670

Silhouette *Desire*

THE WESTMORELANDS

NEW YORK TIMES
bestselling author

BRENDA JACKSON

HOT WESTMORELAND NIGHTS

Ramsey Westmoreland knew better than to lust after the hired help. But Chloe, the new cook, was just so delectable. Though their affair was growing steamier, Chloe's motives became suspicious. And when he learned Chloe was carrying his child this Westmoreland Rancher had to choose between pride or duty.

Available March 2010 wherever books are sold.

Always Powerful, Passionate and Provocative.

Visit Silhouette Books at www.eHarlequin.com

SD73013

SPECIAL EDITION

FROM *USA TODAY* BESTSELLING AUTHOR
CHRISTINE RIMMER

A BRIDE FOR JERICHO BRAVO

Marnie Jones had long ago buried her wild-child
impulses and opted to be "safe," romantically
speaking. But one look at born rebel Jericho Bravo
and she began to wonder if her thrill-seeking side
was about to be revived. Because if ever there was
a man worth taking a chance on, there he was,
right within her grasp....

*Available in March
wherever books are sold.*

Visit Silhouette Books at www.eHarlequin.com

SSE65511

Love Inspired.
SUSPENSE
RIVETING INSPIRATIONAL ROMANCE

Morgan Alexandria moved to Virginia to escape her past...but her past isn't ready to let her go. Thanks to her ex-husband's shady dealings, someone's after her and, if it weren't for Jackson Sharo, she might already be dead. But can Morgan trust the former big-city cop?

HEROES *for* HIRE

RUNNING *for* COVER
by Shirlee McCoy

**Available March
wherever books are sold.**

www.SteepleHill.com

Steeple
Hill®

LIS44384

Devastating, dark-hearted and...
looking for brides.

Look for

BOUGHT: DESTITUTE YET DEFIANT

by *Sarah Morgan*
#2902

From the lowliest slums to Millionaire's Row...
these men have everything now but their brides—
and they'll settle for nothing less than the best!

**Available March 2010
from Harlequin Presents!**

www.eHarlequin.com

HP12902

REQUEST YOUR FREE BOOKS!

2 FREE NOVELS
PLUS
2 FREE GIFTS!

Silhouette®

ROMANTIC SUSPENSE

Sparked by Danger, Fueled by Passion.

YES! Please send me 2 FREE Silhouette® Romantic Suspense novels and my 2 FREE gifts (gifts are worth about $10). After receiving them, if I don't wish to receive any more books, I can return the shipping statement marked "cancel." If I don't cancel, I will receive 4 brand-new novels every month and be billed just $4.24 per book in the U.S. or $4.99 per book in Canada. That's a saving of 15% off the cover price! It's quite a bargain! Shipping and handling is just 50¢ per book in the U.S. and 75¢ per book in Canada.* I understand that accepting the 2 free books and gifts places me under no obligation to buy anything. I can always return a shipment and cancel at any time. Even if I never buy another book from Silhouette, the two free books and gifts are mine to keep forever.

240 SDN E39A 340 SDN E39M

Name	(PLEASE PRINT)	
Address		Apt. #
City	State/Prov.	Zip/Postal Code

Signature (if under 18, a parent or guardian must sign)

Mail to the Silhouette Reader Service:
IN U.S.A.: P.O. Box 1867, Buffalo, NY 14240-1867
IN CANADA: P.O. Box 609, Fort Erie, Ontario L2A 5X3

Not valid for current subscribers to Silhouette Romantic Suspense books.

Want to try two free books from another line?
Call 1-800-873-8635 or visit www.morefreebooks.com.

* Terms and prices subject to change without notice. Prices do not include applicable taxes. N.Y. residents add applicable sales tax. Canadian residents will be charged applicable provincial taxes and GST. Offer not valid in Quebec. This offer is limited to one order per household. All orders subject to approval. Credit or debit balances in a customer's account(s) may be offset by any other outstanding balance owed by or to the customer. Please allow 4 to 6 weeks for delivery. Offer available while quantities last.

Your Privacy: Silhouette is committed to protecting your privacy. Our Privacy Policy is available online at www.eHarlequin.com or upon request from the Reader Service. From time to time we make our lists of customers available to reputable third parties who may have a product or service of interest to you. If you would prefer we not share your name and address, please check here. ☐

Help us get it right—We strive for accurate, respectful and relevant communications. To clarify or modify your communication preferences, visit us at www.ReaderService.com/consumerchoice.

SRS10